GOLD AND SALVATION

Thanks for your help in my writing career. The editing and comments

Enjoy

Gordon Miller

G O R D O N   M I L L E R

GOLD AND SALVATION is a 63,332-word noirish crime novel. It's a tale of murder, love and greed in the border cities of Windsor and Detroit, then down through the States in a 1940 Ford coupe all the way to Juarez, Mexico.

The year is 1952 and it's tough finding an honest job with all the boys back from the war. But Jimmy Delaney figures he's stepped out on Easy Street. He's stolen $60,000 in gold bars—the score of a lifetime. Now all he has to do is haul ass down to Mexico and lay on the beach with Clover Spence: a Mètis woman and the love of his life. Clover is a smart P.I. who's been following the straight and narrow—until she meets Jimmy. What he's done to deserve a dame as fine as Clover he cannot imagine, especially when Easy Street turns into Mean Street. Jimmy's partner is murdered, mobsters want his gold, and the odds of a happy ending start looking mighty slim.

ACKNOWLEDGEMENTS

I wish to express my gratitude to my family and friends for their interest, encouragement and support during the writing of this book

I would also like to thank Brian Henry, editor, writer and creative writing instructor. In addition, members of my Creative Writing Groups for their valuable feedback and enthusiastic assistance.

Thanks to Karen Motherwell for proofreading the manuscript and giving valuable suggestions and healthy criticism.

Special thanks to Ellissa Glad of *Something Creative* for designing the book cover.

CHAPTER 1

1952

It was colder than a mother-in-law's kiss and the damn train was nowhere in sight. Jimmy hadn't been this cold since he was a kid, skating on the pond down the hill from his house with his feet and nose half frozen.

"Where's this goddamn train. I'm up to my ass in snow and it's thirty below, Ray said. "I'm going to light up a smoke."

"No damn way. You know as well as I do we have to stay out of sight. When a chance of a lifetime comes along you have to grab it with both hands and hang on." Jimmy pulled his overcoat collar tight around his neck and covered his ears with his hands. "It won't be long now. I think I heard the whistle."

Swirling snow formed a halo around the single light bulb at the corner of the North Bay station. The wind came in gusts, screamed as it blew around the corners, between the railway station and the freight shed. Passengers could be seen through the station window and a few were standing outside. The only other sound was the faint clicking of Morse code that the telegraph operator was copying. He sat by the window, his green eyeshades down low on his forehead and a cigarette dangling from his lips.

There was an aura of light through the snow in the distance that reflected off the clouds, then the long moan of the engine whistle. Jimmy reached down and picked up the satchel with both hands. He thought he heard Ray's heart pounding, he knew his was.

The snow-covered engine with the bell clanging went by in a cloud of steam. Sparks flew off the wheels as the train screeched to a halt. The timing had to be right on.

Passengers were getting on and off the train. Frost hung in the air in a ghostly reflection of the yellow light from the windows and the long icicles hanging down from the eaves. The telegraph operator unloaded the packages from the express car onto the baggage truck, placing a satchel on top. He bent forward and pulled it though the heavy snow. Jimmy and Ray left the side of the station and walked towards him. Jimmy switched the satchels just as the telegraph operator pulled the baggage truck into the freight shed. He was the only guy who saw them and he was in cahoots. They walked at a slow pace around the station to Ray's Studebaker. Jimmy took the wheel and slowly pulled away through town to Highway 11 and turned north.

"Open it up, Ray."

"Yeah, soon as I thaw out. I'm frozen, can't even move my fingers and I'm still shaking." Ray had the satchel in his lap. He brought his cupped hands to his mouth, breathed heavily on them, than rubbed them together. He took a jackknife out of his pocket, cut the seal on the satchel and slowly opened it. He glanced at Jimmy, reached in and pulled out a bar of gold, then another. "Jesus, we did it!" Ray shouted.

Jimmy jumped up and down in the seat. His hands pounding the steering wheel. "What a score. We're on Easy Street now, buddy."

"I can't believe this. We have a fortune," Ray shouted.

Jimmy reached over, picked up a gold bar and held it out. It glistened from the light of the match that Ray held to light a cigarette. "Just think, it's going to be the life of Riley from now on."

"All we have to do is sell it," Ray said.

"Well, that's your job."

"I know. We'll wait for a few months until this blows over."

"I can't wait, Ray. What are you going to do with your share?"

"I'm going to buy a brand new Cadillac Coupe de Ville, a fucking convertible."

"That'll set you back almost four grand."

"Not only that. I'll buy my girlfriend a fur coat and drive to Toronto to my old man's place and honk the horn. When he comes up I'll holler at him, 'I don't need your money,' and drive away."

Jimmy didn't say anything. He didn't know what he wanted.

The warmth from the heater made the car comfortable. The pent-up excitement gradually left and he felt fatigued. All he had to do was stay awake, take it easy and try to keep the car from sliding into a snow bank. It was going to be a long night but they were almost home free. He thought of his mother, living alone and running the store. Nothing he would have liked better than to stop in and show her the gold. He wasn't a useless son.

He looked over at Ray who was staring out the window into the inky night. "We've been through a lot together. Let's not fuck this up," Jimmy said.

"Nope." Ray continued to look out into the darkness.

The wind had died down and it had stopped snowing by the time they turned off at Englehart. The moon shone, a million stars sparkled and reflected on the snow, as they slowly drove on the icy road to Jimmy's cottage in Wishart Falls

Mile after mile, through the wilderness of Northern Ontario, ghostlike shapes from the tall pine trees stood like sentinels along the road, snow-covered lakes and the faint flicker of the northern lights. Lights in the windows of the cabins and smoke from the chimneys going straight up, from the villages they drove through.

His cottage was a great place to hide the gold until they made arrangements to sell it. He and Ray were the only ones who would know where the gold was hidden, but Ray had no idea how to get there on his own. Jimmy trusted Ray, but not that much. He was kind of a big mouth, especially when he was drunk.

Jimmy slowly drove through Wishart Falls on the recently plowed road and past his mother's store to almost where the highway ended, turned off onto a narrow road and drove through the five inches of snow and parked at the cut-off to the cottage.

"We have to walk from here, buddy," Jimmy said as he reached over and shook Ray's arm.

"I'm awake. Christ, there's two feet of snow. I'll freeze to—"

"I told you to get winter boots and a hat. You city boys are pitiful; pull your socks over your pant legs. Dammit, Ray, this is the easy part. Grab the satchel and let's go."

Jimmy broke trail through the snow to a small shed attached to the cottage. Ray followed. Jimmy kicked away the snowdrift from across the shed door, opened it, took out a shovel, pickaxe, and a potato sack and walked behind the outhouse.

"This is going to take forever," Ray said.

"Quit bitching and put the satchel in the sack." Jimmy shoveled the snow to the bare ground and picked through the frozen earth and stepped back, Ray put the gold in the one-foot deep hole. Jimmy covered it with the chunks of dirt and snow and then smoothed it out.

"Let's get the hell out of here," Jimmy said and walked up the hill to the car. Ray followed. He opened the trunk of the car, took out a five-gallon can of gas and poured it into the gas tank. "I'll drive while you sleep, then we'll change off," he said.

"Okay with me, chum," Jimmy said.

"This is the coldest goddamn country I've ever been in."

"Yeah, let's get back to Windsor. How much do you think the gold's worth?"

"No idea. But I think we're going to be rich for a long time."

Jimmy laughed. He leaned back, stretched out as far as he could on the seat, and fell asleep.

CHAPTER 2

Although Jimmy was back in Windsor, he wasn't so pleased with himself a couple of weeks later when he took the Crosstown bus to Mill and Wyandotte streets. In one way, maybe he should have been even happier, now that he was twice as rich. But some ways to get rich are better than others. The weather hadn't improved, might've even been colder. As Ray would have said, it's cold enough to freeze the ears off a full-grown elephant. But then, Ray wasn't around anymore.

Jimmy looked around to get his bearings then walked down about two houses to a big brick two-story with a small shingle hanging over a door on the corner that read, Smithers Law Office. He knocked. The door opened after a long wait, and there stood Bogart Smithers Jr. He was a little guy, kind of gone to seed, bald, wearing glasses, shirt, tie and a suit that needed cleaning.

"Hey, I know you! You're a dealer at the poker joint," Bogart said.

"I run the place now, but that's me, Jimmy Delaney."

Jimmy followed Bogart down a flight of stairs into a basement office: imitation knotty pine paneling, cement floor and a curtain blocking off the furnace and coal bin. Two desks, four chairs and a filing cabinet made up the furnishings. A calendar was nailed to the wall and a small safe was in a corner. Bogart sat down at a desk that had a telephone, notepads, a couple of files and a newspaper strewn about.

The screaming headline of the newspaper stopped Jimmy in his tracks. He picked it up and quickly read the article as he walked to a chair.

The Toronto Telegram. Jan. 31, 1952.

Gold heist baffles police.

Shock waves reeled through the Canadian Mint yesterday. A shipment that arrived from the goldfields in Timmins, Ontario contained two pieces of sawed off rail. Police reports indicate they were switched for two gold bars moving by rail to Ottawa.

Investigators are concentrating on railway stations in Timmins, North Bay and Ottawa.

Police believe thieves are taking advantage of the lax security displayed in gold shipments from Northern Ontario. This is the latest of three incidents during the last ten years.

Gold is pegged at $35.00 an ounce but experts believe the price could be tripled on the black market due to the huge demand throughout the world.

It appears to be the work of a highly sophisticated gang.

Police say it will be only a matter of time before the case is solved, and offered a $2,000 reward for information leading to an arrest.

Jimmy blushed, tried to suppress a smile and felt a bit of pride. He had never been called sophisticated before or had a price on his head. He turned to Bogart, hoping he hadn't noticed.

"Hello Jimmy, take a seat. Meet Clover, my private investigator."

Leaning against the wall was this dream girl, about thirty, raven black hair piled high on her head, wearing very little makeup and very high heels.

"Hello, Jimmy," she replied. She then walked over, with hips swaying and leaving a trail of perfume, hiked her skirt up and sat on the corner of the desk. All Jimmy saw was her garter belt running down her thigh hooked onto her silk stocking.

Jimmy sat down, averted his eyes, and finally muttered, "Hello." For the first time in his life he didn't know what in hell to say.

"You told me about a murder that concerns you. Sit down and tell me the whole story, everything you can think of." Bogart leaned back, putting his feet on the desk, holding a pen in his left hand, a notepad in his right and a cigar in his mouth.

"Guess some would call it fate, but it looked like bad luck to me," Jimmy said after he finally got his thoughts in order and Clover off his mind.

He started off by telling them about a telephone call from Audrey, an old girl friend. She waited on tables at this beanery he frequented, and also worked as a taxi dancer at a-dime a-dance joint in Detroit, to supplement her income. She told Jimmy she went to visit their friend Ray, one of her former boyfriends, in his downtown apartment. It was a fancy abode in a high rent district. The door was unlocked and when she entered the bedroom, he was in bed and didn't look well. She asked Jimmy to go check him out.

Bogart relit his cigar that smelled like burnt rubber and threw the match in the general direction of the ashtray. Clover walked over and sat at her desk. They were getting interested in the story.

Jimmy took out a package of cigarettes and offered one to Clover. She told him that's one bad habit she doesn't have.

He took one out, put it in his mouth, lit it and continued. Out of breath as he climbed three flights of stairs to Ray's apartment, he entered the living room and kitchen area. He hollered Ray's name and not getting an answer, walked into the bedroom. Except for the blood that ran from the corner of Ray's mouth and the way he laid, you would think he was asleep. A blanket covered him to his neck and one leg dangled over the side of the bed. Jimmy's heart raced. He gasped and took a step back. Anguish surged through him. At times they were like brothers, even when they fought over money and girls. Other than a jealous husband, who would want to kill Ray?

Jimmy hurriedly left the apartment and headed over to Audrey's. Her two-room apartment on Hickory Street was the neatest and cleanest he'd ever seen. A small area rug was always vacuumed and the old linoleum waxed and shiny. Audrey sure kept a clean house. But when you think about it, with a name like Audrey, you would expect her to work at Woolworth's or the library.

"Ray's dead. Why in hell did you set me up like that?" Jimmy hollered as Audrey hesitantly opened the door. "My pal's gone, now I'm involved, and with my record, the cops will be all over me like ketchup on a foot-long hotdog."

"Honest, Jimmy, I didn't know he was dead. There was no one else to turn to so I called you."

Well that hadn't made things any better, but when Jimmy looked at her, loosely covered with a flimsy kimono, legs all the way up to there, and long blonde hair that reminded him of Veronica Lake, it took all the anger out of him. He might add; she was busting out of her tank top. The little gold cross she always wore on a chain around her neck that nestled on her heaving bosom made her look innocent and pure as fresh falling snow.

"The cops won't know if we were there, as long as we didn't leave any evidence," Audrey reasoned.

Jimmy figured he had three options: not do a thing, but then that wasn't right, especially with his best friend murdered. Disguise his voice and call the cops from a pay phone to report it or return to the scene, destroy anything that would leave a trail to him and maybe get a few clues of what in hell happened. He thought of the consequences if a connection was found to the gold caper. "Keep your mouth shut, Audrey. Don't mention this to a soul. I'm going back to Ray's apartment."

"I knew I could depend on you, Jimmy."

Yeah, he thought, as he headed back to the apartment. His partner in crime was murdered. What choice did he have?

Jimmy walked back to Ray's building, entered and walked upstairs. He opened the unlocked door, scanned the kitchen, than stepped in and began a search. He opened a refrigerator that contained a few eggs, a package of lunchmeat and a bottle of ketchup. Two cupboards were barer than Mother Hubbard's. He moved a breadbox on the counter. There were two train tickets, a key and a roll of bills. He pocketed them and continued to the bedroom.

Ray's body was gone!

No, No, it can't be, Jimmy whispered under his breath. His legs felt heavy. He slowly backed out of the bedroom, turned and rushed out of the building.

Bogart said that the story was getting awfully weird and Clover asked who this Ray guy was.

Jimmy took a drink of water out of the glass Clover set down in front of him and went on. Ray got lucky about a year ago. He had this friend Riley, a big lump of a guy with the brains of a chimpanzee, in fact that's what he reminded Jimmy of, and a complete asshole. Trying to be a tough guy and make a name for himself. Some say he had a connection to the Purple Gang in Detroit and it was probably true. He got Ray a job collecting bets from a couple of barbershops and corner stores where they were running numbers. Jimmy thought Ray had skimmed a bit off the top with a little fancy bookkeeping; how else could he afford that apartment?

Jimmy closed his eyes, drummed his fingers on the desk momentarily then continued. Ray was a good-looking dude with blond hair, blue eyes and a smile that would melt a nun's heart. He certainly had a way with the ladies, young and old. Jimmy owed him big time; Ray had helped him through a few bad spells when his finances were low. He wasn't a cheapskate either, bought drinks even if a guy was broke.

Jimmy told them that he ran a weekend poker game for an old buddy. It kept him in walking around money. He still looked for the big score and at twenty-six he sure as hell didn't want to go back to jail. He rented a room in a run down rooming house that wasn't fun either. The landlady was an old family friend from his hometown and seemed to think it was okay to lecture him. Going on and on how he broke his poor widowed mother's heart. How he was raised in a Christian home with all the values that go with it. The problem is what she said was true. It had been a long hard road with more ups and downs than a department store elevator. His luck had been getting better but now things seemed to be falling apart.

Bogart sat up in his chair and put his cigar butt in the ashtray, sat back and asked about Audrey.

Jimmy told them they both came from Wishart Falls, a small town in Northern Ontario where they grew up together. Not much of a future. They left for the bright lights looking for excitement, even a purpose. Anything, to get out of a place they figured had nothing for them. Then Audrey met Ray and Jimmy was history. He still had a connection to the town. His mother lived there. She gave him a small cottage, on a lake, about two miles from town.

Jimmy said he didn't know much about Riley, but his friend Albert Arcand might be able to help. He knew everyone: in fact, he's the guy who suggested that he come and see Bogart.

"I had dealings with Albert a while back; does he still hang out at the Temple Hotel?" Bogart asked.

"He's there most of the time and always on Saturday."

"What exactly do you want me to do, Jimmy?"

Jimmy thought for a minute. How much did he want to tell him? He sure as hell wasn't going to tell him about the gold theft. "Ray and I did a lot of shit together. Maybe the killer's after me too; Ray and I were close friends. I want someone to pay for this."

"Any idea who'd wanted Ray dead?" Bogart asked.

"Other than some husband, I have no idea. He didn't have any enemies that I know of... Well, maybe a few but they wouldn't kill him."

Bogart arched his eyebrows, grinned and rose from his chair. "I'm going to need more information. I'll make an anonymous call to the police. They'll start an investigation. Someone knows something. Get back to me in a week."

Jimmy wrote down his phone number on a notepad on Bogart's desk and put the train tickets and key beside it. He left with the roll of bills in his pocket, and Clover on his mind.

Jimmy had met Albert in the Temple Tavern the day before he visited Bogart. Albert sat by himself over in a corner. Jimmy wandered over, ordered a round of beer on the way. This was the guy he was looking for.

The Temple Hotel had the longest bar in town, even longer than any in Detroit, and was packed with its usual Saturday crowd. Three musicians performed on a stage along the wall across from the bar. The lively yet haunted fiddle melody, The Orange Blossom Special, wafted through the room. The tables along the wall had the usual assortment of hookers, one to a table looking for business. There were young ones, old ones and some in between. Some pretty, some not and some in between. Only thing Jimmy could think of was that a man had lots to choose from. Draft beer at ten cents a glass made things merry, and even though it had been open only two hours, the place was party central.

"You're looking a little peaked today," Albert remarked as Jimmy sat down. With bloodshot eyes, three-day beard, wearing a plaid shirt, khaki pants and an old fedora, Albert didn't look all that great himself. He was an ex con who had been in and out of the slammer since reform school. There was a certain dignity about him and he was held in great esteem by the criminal element. Guess you could say he was a father figure to many of them. He was a real stiff, someone you could rely on when things weren't going as planned. Jimmy needed advice and any help he could get.

"How you doing, Albert?"

"Well, I've seen better days but still kicking."

"Did you know Ray Baxter?"

"What do you mean, did?"

Jimmy told him the whole story about his murder, except the part about Audrey finding the body.

"Jesus," he said, as he slowly reached over, raised his glass of beer and took a long sip. "I'm sorry to hear that. He was a fine young man. We hung around together when serving time in Burwash. He was in for the first time and a bit wet behind the ears. I taught him a few things about cracking safes and staying out of trouble with the screws and more importantly his fellow inmates. Christ, this makes me sad, Jimmy." Albert had a faraway look in his eyes and didn't seem to know what to do with his hands. He traced his finger down the frost on the side of his beer glass. "It's not Kingston, but Burwash could be a dangerous place. Ray told me he came from a well-to-do family. I don't think he gave a damn about anything, just looked for thrills."

Albert pulled a tobacco pouch and cigarette papers from his shirt pocket. His hands shook as he rolled a smoke. He lit it up and continued. "I saw him a couple of months ago. He looked quite prosperous. Nice suit and sitting behind the wheel of a new Chevy, with this sweet thing snuggled up beside him. Introduced me to Ginger, said they were going to get married and he had a big score lined up that would put him on easy street."

"Were you in Kingston Pen?" Jimmy asked. Not mentioning he and Ray were partners in a big score.

"Served four years and six months. I found this so-called friend of mine screwing my girl friend and shot him dead then kicked her the hell out. They both deserved it and I'm not a damn bit sorry." Albert brushed tobacco off the table and his eyes glassed over. "I was quite flush after pulling that big job at the loan company a while back."

"You pulled that job?" Jimmy said. "Christ, that was big time. If I remember right, you had to tunnel in from another building to get to the safe." That was one caper that was talked about many times. It felt good that he trusted him enough to mention it.

"Yep, so I hired a lawyer name of Bogart Smithers Jr. He's a bit of a shyster in my books but he got the charge reduced to manslaughter. It took all my dough, but considering they hung those two guys who murdered a cop last year, I figure it was money well spent."

"I know Bogart, he used to gamble at the poker club," Jimmy said.

"Well, that's his problem. He's not very good at it. Never saw a guy so unlucky. I understand he got into trouble with a loan shark awhile back and got beat up pretty bad." Albert looked down and brushed more tobacco off the table and shook his head. "Someone said he's on the straight and narrow and even quit drinking. He told me he was through a lot in the war. I think he was in the Italian campaign, and has struggled ever since. He knows every cop and crook in town. Has a private dick working with him and conducts his business out of his mother's basement. He should be able to help you."

It was a somber crowd as the guitar player sang Hank Williams' latest hit, Your Cheating Heart. Jimmy and Albert got into some serious drinking and his problems seemed to melt away.

CHAPTER 3

The radiator in the room wasn't much help. Jimmy guessed it was the cold that woke him up. He looked over at the clock, and through the haze, it showed eight o'clock. God knows he didn't want to be awake.

Stained and peeling wallpaper came into focus first. Then a picture of Jesus on the cross that hung on about a forty-five degree angle, like he was leaning over to tell someone off. At least the picture wasn't rocking. When Jimmy blinked a few times it stayed tilted. He figured it was the picture that was wrong, not his brain. Maybe that's why Jesus looked so sorrowful.

"No, it's because of Ray," Jesus said.

"Aw fuck," he muttered. "DTs for sure."

"You shouldn't have killed him, Jimmy."

"I didn't kill him!" But Ray was dead all right. A nasty image of his body floated up on the whiskey fumes in his mind, and he smelled blood and guts.

"Better find out who did that to him," Jesus said.

"Yeah, yeah," Jimmy said, and got up long enough to take a leak and swallow four aspirins. Then he was able to sleep for another four hours.

When he got up for the second time, the clock showed twelve o'clock and it was light out, which meant it was lunch-time, not midnight. At the thought of food his stomach did a slow roll and he had that heavy depressed feeling that comes with the booze. But at least Jesus kept quiet. Jimmy put his pants on and walked down to the bathroom at the end of the hall. The cold water he splashed on his face woke him up. He remembered how much trouble he was in and the more he thought about it; the worse it felt. More cobwebs in his head than a room full of spiders.

He had to figure how to finish the job without Ray. He set it up but Ray had the connections to sell the gold. Where the hell did the body disappear to and why? When he really thought about it, why was Ray dead and not he? Ray was just a happy-go-lucky kid, didn't give a damn about anything: booze, broads and a good time were all that mattered. They were close; maybe he should've taken care of him. He might be next and his fingerprints are all over Ray's apartment. All Jimmy needed was to get involved with the cops. There'd been no recent news about the gold theft but he was damn sure no one had forgotten it. He was going to have to sell the gold and he had no idea how. Only thing he knew about finance was how to spend money.

Jimmy pulled a few bills out of his pocket. He was damn near broke, just enough for cigarettes, and he needed a drink in the worst way. He hoped his credit was good at Booker T's because it was a long time until the poker joint opened at eight.

It was only a couple of blocks to a bootlegger. There were two guys that sat at a table sipping beer, talking hockey and looking like they hadn't slept for days. Guess they were out on the town last night like he was. Hope the poor bastards didn't have his problems.

"What'll you have Jimmy?" Booker asked. He wasn't all that big but he sure looked powerful with his gold tooth, bald-head and handlebar moustache. The man was a sight to behold. He was a washed-up prizefighter, boxed out of Detroit not that long ago. Jimmy heard he was a middleweight contender and fought on the same card as Joe Louis at Madison Square Garden. Booker injured his eye in a match and had to quit.

"I'm a little short of scratch today, Booker, sicker than a dog. Would like a few drinks on credit."

"Damn it Jimmy. You owe me now, when you going to pay up?"

"I swear on my dear old mother's grave, Booker, when I get paid Saturday this will be my first stop."

"I thought you told me your mother was still alive?"

"Damn, who in hell gives a shit? That's what you call a figure of speech, Booker." He wasn't all that happy but served Jimmy a beer anyway, making a ham sandwich to go with it.

Some said he was a bit punch drunk from all the pounding he'd taken in the ring, and the high living. He used to party around in all the high class joints with a woman on each arm. They all left with the money and fame.

The fog started to lift after the third beer, and things got a bit clearer. If Jimmy was going to help catch Ray's killer he figured he had to find Ginger, this girlfriend of Ray's. He'd met her but all he remembered is that she was a looker with flaming red hair.

"Thanks, Booker," Jimmy said as he was leaving.

"Oh by the way, Jimmy," Booker hollered, "Couple of guys from Detroit in asking about you yesterday. They were a couple of mean looking bastards."

The two guys that sat at the table stared at Jimmy, one made the sign of the cross. Jimmy's stomach started to hurt all over again and his heart skipped so many beats he thought it was going to stop. Those Detroit bastards had to be from the Purple Gang. This was the mob that controlled Michigan, parts of Ohio and the Windsor area. They must have heard something. He was in deep shit.

Jimmy was one nervous bastard as he headed over to Pitt Street in the early evening. Now it wasn't only the cops he had to worry about, there were these Detroit hoods. This is the part of town where Ray used to hang out with the fast crowd. It was a good place to start looking for Ginger. Chances are she frequented the place.

Like all border towns this was an area that attracted the bad guys from all over, big time and small time crooks to war veterans who craved the excitement from their army days.

Some of the Yankees that flooded in from across the border were hard bastards. Only time Jimmy frequented the area was for the best Chinese food in town.

When he entered White's Tavern the music from the juke-box was playing Theresa Brewer's, *Till I Waltz Again With You*. The red-colored lights hanging from the ceiling were turned down, and one couple danced real close on the small dance floor.

A redhead sat at the bar all by herself; she looked for-lorn, and sipped on what looked to Jimmy like a Singapore Sling. What the hell, a faint heart never won fast ladies. "Hi Ginger, remember me?" She turned, and gave him a look that was colder than Northern Ontario in the month of January.

"Yeah, I remember, you're Jimmy. My boyfriend, Ray, talked a lot about you and how you were both going to get rich." Her speech was slurred. She was about half way to being smashed.

"What else did he say?"

"That's about all. He hasn't called in days and I'm starting to get worried." He had big plans and I went with them."

"Did he say what those plans might be?"

"You're awful nosy. Just leave me alone."

He decided he had to change tactics and asked her to dance. Well, he was not going to say what she told him to do, but figured he better leave. As he was halfway to the door she shouted "If you see Ray, tell him to call me right away."

"Yeah, okay." He didn't tell her that Ray would never call.

He continued on his long walk to the rooming house. Thoughts of Ray kept entering his mind. This was the kind of evening they would get together in one of the taverns along Drouillard Road, drink beer and talk about sports, women, friends, enemies and lost and future opportunities. He entered his room, kicked off his shoes, stretched out on the bed and fell into a troubled sleep.

The next morning, Jimmy was surprised as hell when the phone rang around ten. He never got calls on Saturday morning.

"Good morning, Jimmy. How's my favorite client?" It was Clover! Her voice gave him shivers, and his sadness disappeared. How lucky did a guy have to be to have someone like Clover calling?

"I would like to meet with you Jimmy, off the record. Can you be at Thomas's Inn, say about two this afternoon?"

He damn near fell over. Hell yes, he thought to himself, he'd meet her anywhere and anytime.

"Yeah, OK, I'll be there." He tried to sound hip. No way would she be interested in him.

After about a mile walk he arrived a bit early. What was on her mind?

The inn was an old roadhouse speakeasy, famous during prohibition and the rum-running days, catering to rich Americans: the Dodges, Fords, Jack Dempsey, Al Capone and big league ball players to name a few. There were great dinners of seafood, chicken and frog legs served in the fancy dining room and gambling and dancing upstairs––all before Jimmy's time, but still talked about with reverence whenever old-timers got together for a drink. He never tired of hearing the stories.

He walked in through to the back door and watched the parking lot out of the side window. An old Ford coupe pulled in and drove over to a far corner. The door opened and out stepped Clover, a black hat with a wide brim slightly tilted to the side, a fur coat that reached below her knees, and red shoes. Have to say it again; she's a real dish. She had Ava Gardner all beat to hell.

"Good to see you, Clover," he said when she walked in.

"Let's go sit down, Jimmy, I'll buy you a drink." She took his hand and smiled. They walked to a table in a far corner of the bar. A couple of the regulars got whiplash when they turned to look at her.

The waiter brought over their drinks and, with a flourish, set down a Manhattan in front of Clover; he then reached over with a bottle of Cincinnati Cream, Jimmy's favorite beer.

"Jimmy, when you came into the office the other day, you turned red and your chest went out about six inches when you saw the headlines in the paper, picked it up and read the story about the two bars of gold stolen in North Bay. I thought you were going to faint. Bogart never mentioned it so I don't think he suspects anything. I think you and Ray were involved." She brought her drink up to her lips, and peered over the glass with those big brown bedroom eyes.

Jimmy stuttered and stammered. After gulping down half his beer he said, "Jesus, you sure know how to get to the point," while he tried to buy time and think of what to say.

"If it can be assumed my suspicions are true, give it some hard thought. I've been around the block a few times, Jimmy, and have connections. Think it over and if you want to talk, give me a call at my apartment. Just look up the number in the phone book." With that, she put on her coat and sashayed out the door. Jimmy finished his drink, her drink and ordered another.

This was a way out but could he trust her?

CHAPTER 4

1946

Jimmy shivered in his light jacket as he looked up at the clouds drifting across the sky that played hide and seek with the full moon. The light reflected off Audrey's face. They sat side by side on the station platform. They sipped on a bottle of Four Aces, a forty-nine cent bottle of sherry that cost three dollars at the bootleggers. Jimmy laughed when Audrey giggled from the effects of the wine. Feelings of sadness and despair seemed to disappear.

Saturday night in Jimmy's hometown of Wishart Falls didn't have much in the line of excitement. The only sound was a dog barking. The only light came from the windows of the Tasty Lunch, the Bissonnette Tavern and the poolroom. They cast a yellow glow onto the wooden sidewalks. It was the typical one-horse town in the north. A railroad ran though it; there were two sawmills, two lumber camps and a depleted gold mine. A dusty main street surrounded by a movie theatre, the post office, a restaurant, two poolrooms, two beer parlors, a barbershop and a general store added to the landscape. A few businesses, including Jimmy's mothers small grocery store, sat over on a side street, with the Catholic and Protestant churches and schools that attempted to educate the children and get them a ticket to heaven.

"Have another drink," he said as he passed the bottle to Audrey.

"Why not, I'm in shit at home as it is. My dad will be working on his sermon, mom reading *True Romance*, and both waiting to chew me out. All about having to set an example to the kids in town and to live a good life, while he does the Lord's work. I can't even wear lipstick and if I don't pass grade twelve…I'm done for."

He knew her father told her to stay away from him. And although he was seriously tempted, it was hands off. She had problems enough.

"It hasn't been the same since my Dad died," Jimmy said. "Some say it was a suicide. All I know is they pulled him out of the lake after dragging for three days. Sitting on the bank of the lake, I cried like a baby as I watched boats dragging big hooks along the bottom and firing shotguns. They say the vibrations get the body to rise to the surface. Guess it does, they found him."

"I'm sorry, Jimmy. I remember him from the store. When we bought candy, he'd throw in a few extra."

"He'd sit in his chair with the lights out for days on end. Ma would rant and rave but it didn't seem to matter. They started up the store about twenty-five years ago, shortly after he came back from the war. He never talked about it but I heard he was wounded somewhere in France," Jimmy said as he zippered up his jacket, opened a package of cigarettes and offered one to Audrey.

"No thanks. That's all I need to do is smell smoke. Well, maybe I'll take a few drags off yours."

"I should quit. My mother's going to notice cigarettes missing from the store one of these days. She wants me to take over the store."

"You'd make one hell of a storekeeper," she laughed. "I want to be a nurse. They wear those cute caps with a blue stripe and I'd like to help people."

"One thing about it, we both want to leave town and head for the bright lights."

"I better get home. Hope my parents are gone to bed." She got up, buttoned up her sweater, walked away then turned and said, "See you later, alligator."

Jimmy drank the last of the wine and watched her disappear into the darkness.

He had been out of town once, well twice, but a train ride of twenty miles to Westree to play ball didn't really count. He remembered looking at the neon lights in front of the shops and restaurants in Sudbury. More pretty girls than he had ever seen before, sidewalks full of people, and cars and taxis moving up and down the streets. He wanted to be part of that life. Maybe even get to Toronto.

He walked home and tiptoed into his bedroom.

A cool breeze was blowing through the open door, when Jimmy walked out of his bedroom, and into the store the next morning. The shelves along the walls were filled with grocery items, everything from canned goods to bags of flour. There was a glass counter filled with candy and chocolate bars. A pop machine on one side and an old brass cash register on a corner of the counter, where his mother sat on a stool working on a ledger. A pencil was stuck behind her ear and her grey hair hung down over her eyes. Wearing a big smock over her housedress and scruffy shoes made her seem old and frail. Guess she was having it rough too.

They lived in four rooms in back of the store: a kitchen, two bedrooms and a small sitting room. His bedroom, with the flowered wallpaper and the pine floor, was furnished with a cot, a dresser, a small table and a chair. A model airplane hung from the ceiling and his .22 caliber rifle was between two pegs on the wall. His clothes hung from nails in a board that was next to his bed. The room was his refuge. He didn't know why but it was the only place he felt at peace.

He walked into the kitchen and sat at the table. His mother placed a box of Kellogg's cornflakes down. "Get yourself a bowl and cup while I make tea."

Jimmy didn't say anything. He sat with his elbows on the table and silently read the writing on the cereal box. His mother looked at him and said, "I know you're not happy son. You're only eighteen but think about it, you're one of the lucky ones, a job at the sawmill, and eating well at home. That's more than a lot of the young people around town. It's not the same since your father died, God bless his tortured soul."

"I miss him a lot, Ma."

"You were the apple of his eye, son. It's over now and we have to make the best of it. We're fairly well off with the store and the cottage." She put a tablespoon of tea in the teapot, filled it with boiling water, placed it on the table and sat down opposite him.

"How in the world did you and Dad end up in this god-forsaken place?"

"I was sixteen. I came with my parents in 1917. My father was the bookkeeper for the lumber company."

"What about Dad?"

She sipped her tea and smiled. "He came shortly after and got a job in the sawmill. We met at the skating rink. Oh, he was a wonderful skater. He was the best hockey player on our team. The railroad has just been built and lumbering and mining started up. We were married shortly after and scrimped and saved. When we had enough to buy a few groceries, and convert our parlor into a store, we were in business. Those were happy days, son." Her eyes turned opaque and her lips tightened. "Then the demons came and your father changed."

"Is that when he started drinking?"

"Shortly after. He tried hard not to, but once he started even the good Lord couldn't stop him."

His mother took Jimmy's lunch pail off the shelf and packed two bologna sandwiches, cookies, an apple and a bottle of pop. She then put her smock on and walked out into the store.

At least she didn't get into how Jimmy started to swear, sass her, not listen and how disappointed she was when he got kicked out of school. He left the house and walked the half-mile to the sawmill, ready for the day shift.

"Hey, Audrey." Jimmy shouted when she walked past the store a few days later. She looked away, hesitated, then turned to Jimmy and removed her headscarf. Her right cheekbone was purple and swollen. Her lip had a slight cut.

"Jesus, what happened?" He took her hand and led her to the swing in the backyard. She sat on the seat and held the rope. Jimmy gently pushed it.

"I failed grade twelve and my father beat me. He said I brought shame on the family." Her sobs seemed to come from some deep well and she fought for breath. "I don't know what to do. I did the best I could."

"The son-of-a-bitch. What did your mother say?"

"Oh, she cried but didn't dare say anything."

"Let's leave this damn town, there's nothing for us here," Jimmy said and took her hand.

She stepped back and looked up at him. "Yes, I can't stand it anymore."

"There's no turning back, Audrey. Do you really want to go?"

"Yes."

"There's a suitcase at the cottage, that's where we'll bring our stuff."

"Okay, meet me on the road at the edge of town after dark tonight and we'll walk there. I'll have my clothes," Audrey said. "My parents are going out tonight."

"I'll bring mine too," Jimmy said.

Audrey didn't say anything. She got up from the swing and walked home.

A new moon was rising and casting enough light to see the road. Jimmy left through the back door, carrying a shopping bag, and walked to the road leading off to the cottage, where Audrey was waiting. Jimmy gave her a cigarette and took one for himself. He saw a smile on her face from the light of the match.

"I don't know what this will bring but I can't wait to leave," she said.

Jimmy put his arm around her waist as they walked to the cottage in the darkness each carrying a shopping bag.

Jimmy lit the kerosene lamp, set it on the kitchen table and walked into the bedroom for the suitcase. He opened it up on the couch and Audrey started packing.

"We're going to have to leave a few things behind, there's not that much room," she said.

"Leave mine, I don't need that much."

"You're so nice, Jimmy."

Her face was flushed and her hands shook when she finished and turned to Jimmy. He embraced her and their lips sought each other. There wasn't a word spoken. She undressed and sat on the bed. He fumbled with his belt, took his pants and shirt off, lay on the bed and pulled her down beside him.

Two days later, after the sun disappeared behind the trees, Jimmy rode his bike out to the cottage for the suitcase and hid it in his room. Later, just before he went to bed he sat at the table and wrote a letter.

> *Dear Ma,*
>
> *I'm leaving here and going to Windsor. They say there is a lot of work there. I took my money out of the jar where I've been saving it.*
>
> *Audrey is going too. Things aren't going well at her place. Please tell her mother that I will take care of her. I will write.*
>
> *Your loving son, Jimmy.*

The bus stopped in front of the hotel in the early evening the next day. Audrey and Jimmy left the shelter of the entrance, ran through the rain, and boarded.

It was hot and stifling, the sidewalks were scorched when Jimmy and Audrey got off the bus in Windsor. Jimmy carried a beat-up suitcase, two hundred dollars in his pocket and the address of a rooming house. They lived in one room on the second floor.

Work was plentiful. His job in a factory that manufactured automobile radiators didn't pay much, but combined with the money from Audrey's waitress job, it was enough to get by. The rent for the room was cheap and they borrowed a small hot plate from the landlady to boil water, warm up and fry food. With their newfound freedom they were happy.

They usually spent Friday night in one of the many bars on Drouillard Road and that's when Ray entered their lives.

Jimmy noticed Audrey's eyes widen when she turned towards the door. He turned to look. A guy with blond wavy hair, wearing a suit and tie, stood at the door and looked around. It was probably Audrey's smile that brought him over to their table.

"The place is crowded, mind if I sit here?" He signaled to the waiter for a round of beer and sat down. He shook Jimmy's hand, put his hand on Audrey's shoulder and said, "I'm Ray Baxter."

"I'm Jimmy and this is Audrey, we're new in town and just started working." He looked over at Audrey. Her eyes seemed to smolder and she had a smile a mile wide as she stared at Ray.

"About the same here. Only I'm not working. I think there are better opportunities to make a living."

That's when Jimmy's life of crime began.

Guess Ray wasn't to blame, but it sure looked suspicious when the cops raided Jimmy and Audrey's apartment one Sunday morning. After a search, they found a few pieces of jewelry under his mattress. Somebody must have squealed on him. The stealing sounded easy, when he and Ray started to break into jewelry stores. It was the excitement more than anything else, because they blew the money as fast as they got it. Flashy clothes and the respect Jimmy got from his new friends made him feel big.

Sitting in a jail cell and time in the exercise yard were boring. Tougher yet was the shame he felt. Especially after getting letters from his mother pleading with him to come home.

When he was released from Don Jail, after serving three months, he returned to his room and found Audrey's clothes gone. He had a damn good idea where she went. He should have known. Looking back there was a change in her attitude towards him recently and she didn't visit him in jail. Ray could get any girl he wanted. For some reason or other it didn't bother Jimmy that much. Audrey and he were more like friends than lovers. Besides, he and Ray had really hit it off. Guess they could be called birds of a feather. They didn't worry about tomorrow. Everything was fun and games. He didn't think anyone could hold a grudge against Ray, didn't matter what the hell it was. He could charm anyone.

Ray and Jimmy shared a cell in Guelph Reformatory a little later. They got caught stealing copper wire from along a railway line. It sounded like a good idea at the time. Jimmy convinced George, a railroad lineman and drinking buddy, to loan him his climbers, belt, wire cutters and to show him how to use them. They had to be quick. A repair crew would be out as soon as communications went down.

They drove to a remote section of a railway, parked and walked through a cornfield to the tracks. Jimmy strapped the climbers to his boots, fastened the belt to his waist and around the pole.

"Jesus, I thought you knew how to do it," Ray said, after Jimmy's third attempt to climb.

"It's a hell of a lot harder than it looks. I think I'm getting the hang of it." Finally he edged up the pole to the copper wire, cut five strands and climbed down. They hurried over to the next pole. Jimmy fell on the first two tries, took the loose climbers off and strapped them on again.

"Dammit, Jimmy. This is taking too long," Ray said.

Jimmy was half way up the pole when the light of a flashlight shone on him and then Ray. A railroad cop had his gun drawn and pointed at Ray. Two railroad employees stood in the shadows.

"You're both under arrest," the cop said, quickly handcuffed Ray and nabbed Jimmy when he climbed down.

They spent the night in the town jail and appeared before a magistrate the next morning. They pleaded guilty and each received an eight-month sentence.

The only good thing he could say about the jail was that he got an education in the art of thievery. With a little bit of advice from a couple of old-timers, he and Ray revised their plan for the gold robbery.

CHAPTER 5

Jimmy hoped the second meeting Bogart called would clear up a few things. It had gotten worse. The Detroit mobsters were after him. He didn't see any headway with Ray's murder and where did his body end up? Another thing that worried Jimmy were the cops. The only good thing going was the gold he had hidden, but how in hell was he going to sell it? That's what Ray was going to do.

The bowl of cut flowers on Clover's desk and curtains on the window brightened up Bogart's office. Can't say the same about his desk; it looked like a cyclone had touched down just after his bowl of soup was placed on it, leaving tomato stains and cracker crumbs over everything including his tie.

A voice from upstairs called "Do you want your coffee now?"

"Yes, Mother, please bring three," Bogart said, than turned to Jimmy. "Sit yourself down, Good to see you."

A classy looking dame, her gray hair tinted blue and dressed in a black suit came downstairs and set the coffee down. Bogart introduced his mother.

"How do you do, Mrs. Smithers," Jimmy said.

"Hello. Just call me Belle and I'll call you Jimmy."

She turned and looked at Bogart. "I'm going out to play bridge, Dear. I'll be back in time to cook supper."

Bogart seemed to wince, "Okay Mother."

With the phone at her ear and wearing a yellow sundress, Clover looked like a secretary at work; but when she put the phone down and started to speak, there was no doubt in anyone's mind, she was one smart lady in charge of this investigation.

"Ray's body is nowhere to be found, but he sure got himself into trouble with the mob. According to information from Bogart's sources, he pocketed some of the money from the betting slips," Clover said.

"No damn wonder. You don't screw around when you're dealing with these guys," Jimmy said.

"Well, this good customer," Clover explained, "produced his numbers for a three-hundred dollar prize and there was no record of it. The barber who took the bet says he gave it to Ray. Riley was on his case to get the money back and I'm sure Ray didn't have it. Not only is it hurting Riley's reputation, he has to pay back the dough."

Bogart cut in, "This shouldn't affect you, Jimmy."

Like hell it doesn't, Jimmy thought. Did Ray mention he'd pay it back with some big score he lined up? Riley might be dumb but he runs the mob in Windsor. He's a crafty son-of-a-bitch and he knows Ray and Jimmy are partners in crime.

"Yeah, and I wonder what big promises he made?" Jimmy said.

"There seems to be a lot of talk about that gold caper. Guys putting two and two together and figure it might be a local gang. Right now we're at a dead end but it's starting to get int‸resting," Bogart said and stood up. "Clover has a few ideas on how to continue our investigation. Give me a call in about a week. I expect a payment then too, Jimmy."

Jimmy took a side-glance at Clover on his way out the door, thought she winked at him. He whistled a tune as he left and headed to work at the gambling joint. It was a small residence on Felix Avenue near a bus stop. A light fixture hung over each of the two tables. All you could hear were the low voices of the seven guys at each one. A few others sat around drinking beer, and listening to a ballgame on the radio, in a small room off to the side. The action and the excitement, along with the smell of booze, heavy cigarette smoke, and the sense of anticipation gave most of them a rush. Friday night was usually the busiest of the week. Blackjack and seven-card-stud were the games of choice. Jimmy kept order, served beer and kept his eye on the dealers who took the rake-off. He hoped things kept going smoothly. Most of these guys were poor suckers who were never going to win in the long run. The card sharks were okay guys, they didn't want to be banned; this was their livelihood. It was the criminal element that concerned him. Some were hard as nails, usually carrying knives and the odd pistol, and not afraid to use them.

Riley was at the blackjack table, losing heavily, bragging about his connections and was his usual obnoxious self. He usually had one of his underlings with him so he really didn't care who he rubbed the wrong way.

Jimmy hoped he would leave all this behind soon. His dream of sitting on a beach in Mexico, drinking tequila might even come true.

Finally, about seven in the morning the last two card players left. Jimmy kicked out a couple of guys leaning back sleeping in their chairs, locked up and headed over to Booker's. He was too damn keyed up to sleep. Booker was usually up and his place open by this time. He served the odd hung-over customer on Saturday morning.

The only customer was a woman sitting at a table, sipping on a drink that looked like rye and ginger. A new hairdo and stylish clothes offset her puffy eyes and sunken cheeks. She must have been a beauty about twenty years ago.

"Hey Booker, How much am I into you for?"

"Jesus Jimmy, you know I don't keep track. Just give me what you owe."

Jimmy made a rough calculation in his head and gave him ten dollars. "That's half, I have to save some to pay my lawyer."

"Jesus, stay away from those guys, they're a bunch of crooks. What one you dealing with?"

"Smithers, I think he's an OK guy."

"Hell, I know his mother, Belle; a fine woman. Ran a blind pig during Prohibition. Used to have a few girls working for her. I was her best customer back in the good old days. Jesus

Jimmy, you should've been around then. It's all gone now but I wouldn't trade those days for the world. I was a contender, Jimmy, damn near champion of the world."

There was something about these old guys, hard as nails and living on the edge, used the few talents they were blessed with to make their way in the world, and not ask for anything but a chance.

CHAPTER 6

1940

Eighteen-year-old Clover Spence sat with her grandfather on the front porch of the family farmhouse, under the powder blue skies and wheat fields that seemed to go on forever. It shimmered like gold under the early evening sun. She dreamt of a world she would soon become part of, only half paying attention to her grandfather's tales of long ago. They were the Métis, descendants of the French voyageurs and Scottish fur traders who married Indian women and lived in the Red River Settlement in total freedom. They were self reliant and strong. Huge herds of buffalo roamed these plains. They hunted them on horseback for food and clothing. He told her of the great hunters and warriors who came before them. They had fought for independence under Louis Riel, their political and spiritual leader; also Gabriel Dumont, a farmer, trader and buffalo hunter who led the rebellion and was defeated. Now they plow the fields like ordinary men.

"You must bring your dream catcher," her grandfather said, "it used to hang over your bed when you were a baby."

"I don't remember it," Clover replied.

"I've kept it safe. Your grandmother made it for you when you were born.' He handed it to her. It was a tear-shaped willow frame with sinew strands made into a web. A few beads were sewn in and a raven feather hung down from the bottom. The webbing was broken in places and the feather bent and soiled. Clover knew they were made by grandmothers to hang over a sleeping child to catch the bad dreams that entangled in the web. Only the good dreams filtered through and traveled down the feathers to the sleeping baby. It would protect them from nightmares and bring them harmony with their surroundings.

"Your mother and father are very sad to see you go. I told them you wanted to see the outside world and your dream of getting an education. I can see you are not happy here."

"I saw an ad in the paper asking for women to work in the war plants. They make good money. She blushed, "Then, I want to be a school teacher."

"Please come back some day. I am old but hope to see you again. Stay true to the teachings of our people."

She placed her hand on his arm and said, "I will." Why would she do otherwise?

She boarded the train at Winnipeg. She wore her new cashmere sweater, plaid skirt and straw hat. With her high school diploma tucked in her purse she felt ready to take on the world. Her mother cried softly as she hugged her. Her father looked sad and bewildered when he took her hands and kissed her on the cheek. Their only child was setting out to find a better life, and fulfill her dreams, in the far-off cities of Ontario.

It was a three-day train ride, sitting in a crowded day coach, eating her lunches from home then ham and cheese sandwiches from the newsie. The only break was leaving the train at various stops along the way for a few short minutes. The clicking of the passenger coach wheels on the rails would lull her into a light sleep. The smells from unwashed passengers and cigarette smoke seemed to dissipate after the first day. A soldier strummed a guitar and sang a country song. Some were talking and laughing; others were playing cards or sleeping. Fending off advances from soldiers, on leave or assignment traveling across the country, added to her woes. The lonesome wail of the engine whistle blowing at train crossings brought memories of home. She fought a twinge of homesickness and regret.

Clover finally arrived in Toronto and started to work in a war plant. The Great Depression had made things long and lean in the prairies but with the war starting there was opportunity: travel and jobs. With her looks, ambition and sense of adventure, there were better things ahead.

Even with a shortage of men she had her choice of almost anyone she wanted. She soon tired of the world of parties and dancing.

The house band was playing Paper Doll and the Palais Royale was filling up; it was Saturday night. Clover was standing at the counter buying a bottle of pop.

"Can I have the next dance?" He looked at her, averted his eyes and his face flushed.

"Sure, as soon as I finish my drink," Clover said. He was about as tall as she was and looked sophisticated but weary in his blue suit, white shirt and blue and gold-stripped tie.

"I'm Clover Spence."

"Bogart, Bogart Smithers, nice to meet you. I'm not much of a dancer."

"Oh that's okay." She swallowed a large drink of pop, put the bottle down and said, "Let's go."

He was right about the dancing. She had a sore toe. "Let's go sit. I'm tired. I had a hard day." They walked as far from the dance floor as they could and sat down.

"So, what do you do, Bogart?"

"I'm just back on Civvie Street and starting law school."

"The war's not over yet."

'It is for me. My leg's full of shrapnel. I'm no damn good for them anymore. They sent me home. Maybe we can try dancing again when a slow piece comes on."

"I have a better idea, let's go to a restaurant and have a bite?"

Clover liked him. He seemed quite serious. She knew he was too damn shy to ask her out. "Maybe we can meet again sometime," she said and wrote her phone number down and gave it to him. Maybe it was time she settled down.

They shared a club sandwich and drank coffee. Bogart paid the bill and drove Clover home.

Clover felt at peace, instead of having this continual search for excitement and fun. It wasn't love, maybe just a fondness for Bogart and a choice of a stable life. After a brief courtship, he asked her to move in with him, she accepted. From helping him with his law courses, she soon knew almost as much about it as he did. She didn't know what was coming.

Soon after he graduated from law school they moved to Bogart's hometown of Windsor. She liked the place, a factory town with a population of 120,000. It was a good place to build a future. He set up a law practice and she started to work at a factory that made car brakes. They lived with his mother Belle; that was a mistake. She ran Bogart, the household and tried to run Clover.

Bogart's fledging law practice soon grew, so did his drinking. She didn't know what demons Bogart lived with; at times he was raving drunk, or gambling: horses and cards. After nursing him through a case of the DTs, then a severe beating from a loan shark, Clover had enough of Bogart and Belle. She left and moved into an apartment with a co-worker.

That seemed to wake up Bogart and after being on the straight and narrow for six months, straightening out his debts, business was back to normal and he needed help. Clover agreed to work for him as an office assistant and private investigator.

CHAPTER 7

Jimmy was leaning over the kitchen sink in his room, eating a cucumber sandwich, when he heard a solid knock on the door. Who in hell was that, he thought.

"Jimmy, are you home?"

Jimmy recognized the voice, unlocked and opened the door.

There stood Sergeant O'Connor, meanest bastard on the police force. He drove more than one of Jimmy's friends down to the waterfront for a form of frontier justice. He was a bit on the chunky side and you could smell the brylcream in his hair, plastered across his head, trying to cover his bald spot. Don't think his suit was ever dry-cleaned.

"What can I do for you, Sarge?" Jimmy didn't invite him in but he entered anyway, and took a fast look around.

"You can't just walk in like this. You need a warrant."

"Relax, Jimmy. This is a social visit."

"I'm going to talk to my lawyer about this."

"The department got an anonymous call and I got a call from a landlord about your old buddy Ray. It seems he's been missing for a while and upon our investigation, we found blood on his bed sheets and your fingerprints all over the place. Would you care to enlighten me on what you know?" O'Connor put his hands in his pockets and leaned back on the wall. "You're in deep shit Jimmy, come clean and I'll try and give you a break."

Never enlighten a cop; they'll hang you with it if they get a chance. "I don't know a damn thing and I visit him at times; so I'm sure I left fingerprints around the place. Beside, this is news to me and we were pretty close friends," Jimmy said, trying to appear sad. That wasn't hard to do because he was also scared as hell. "Ray was my chum, you know that, we did a hell of a lot together."

"Yeah, like robbing people, and spending time in jail." He grinned. "I have your number, Jimmy."

"I'm on the straight and narrow now."

"They all say that. We'll be in touch, Jimmy, and don't leave town." O'Connor reached into his shirt pocket for a cheap White Owl cigar, unwrapped it, put it in his mouth and left.

Jimmy threw the crust from his sandwich into a garbage bag and sat down on his sagging bed. He was getting deeper and deeper into a real mess. Being guilty or innocent doesn't matter much when you're a lawbreaker and jailbird. Maybe he should go home, to the small village he came from and work with his mother in the grocery store, but no damn way would he do that. He liked it just fine where he was. There was excitement in Windsor. The city of Detroit was a ten-cent bus ride away with big league sports, bars open on Sunday and pretty women. Then there was Clover, a beautiful woman he'd just met, and hopefully would get to know better, and most important of all, two bars of gold.

Jimmy dialed his lawyer. He needed legal advice fast.

"Smithers law office, Bogart speaking."

"This is Jimmy, a visitor just left. It was Sergeant O'Connor. They're looking into Ray's disappearance. He came waltzing into my place like he owned it"

"What did you tell him?"

"Not a damn thing, just what you told me to do."

"Good, You know as well as I do to keep your mouth shut. Clover's been working on the case and figures whoever murdered Ray weren't the same ones who moved the body.

"How does she figure that?"

She says the mob would have done it when they shot him."

"Well, who in hell did?"

"That's what you're paying me to find out."

"They found my prints all over the place."

"That doesn't prove a damn thing Jimmy. Just lay low and don't lose your head."

Easy for him to say, it's not his ass on the line.

The pavement was almost bare and small rivulets from the melting snow ran, hugging the curb, to a drain. A couple of small boys were making dams and small canals to divert the water. A robin flew by with a beak full of straw to an elm tree.

Everyone had a spring in their step and seemed glad to be alive.

Jimmy didn't feel that way when he walked down the street from the bus stop and entered the dreary and dark atmosphere of the Temple Tavern. Guess he had the Monday morning blues. The place was damn near empty and sitting over in his usual corner, nursing a beer and reading *The Windsor Star*, was Albert.

He looked up as Jimmy approached, "Hey, Jimmy."

"Good morning, Albert, how's it hanging?"

His eyes narrowed, as he looked Jimmy up and down, as if he knew something Jimmy didn't or something Jimmy didn't want him to know.

"Interesting article today, Jimmy," and passed him the front section of the paper.

Jimmy read the article, printed in the lower left hand side of the front page, and tried to look nonchalant. Inside he was as nervous as a virgin on her wedding night: they knew they were going to get it but didn't know how.

According to a Provincial Police spokesman, police are concentrating their search for the stolen Timmins gold shipment in the North Bay area. A railway employee was brought in for questioning and is being named a material witness.

Investors say if the thieves sell the gold on the black market, it would be an approximate $60,000 windfall. Because of the scope and magnitude of the heist, and *inside knowledge required, police think there may be an International connection.*

Albert waited until the waiter set down two beers, looked around and back at Jimmy. "Well, whoever pulled this job were pretty smart boys. Took a lot of brains and guts," Albert said.

"It sure as hell did," Jimmy muttered. What in hell did he get into, and why is Albert so interested?

"I've been thinking quite a bit about Ray," Albert said. "He didn't have to live a life of crime. He was born into a life of riches and opportunity, and when I think about it, neither did you."

"I wasn't born rich."

"You still had the chance to get an education and become something." Albert rolled a cigarette, lit it and continued, "You young bucks today have it too easy. Why, back in my day if you didn't work, you starved."

Jimmy laughed. He wasn't going to contradict him.

Albert continued, "I didn't have much opportunity in life, came from a fucked-up family in the hills of Kentucky. Moonshining was a way of life and practiced for generations." His eyes glazed over as he stared at his beer. He finished it and raised the glass at the waiter, signaling for another round. "I drove booze from the stills to the distributors throughout the mountains, starting at age fifteen; got caught and sent to reform school. Try and get a half-assed job when folks around the area learned that."

"So, what did you do?"

"Kept on driving, even though it was damn dangerous. The revenuers shooting at you and hair spin turns to maneuver. Lot of the boys ended upside down on the bottom of a mountain. My old dad was one of them."

Geez, there was no stopping Albert when he started to reminisce. Jimmy heard it all before but enjoyed it anyway.

"My uncle took me under his wing, and during his few periods of freedom, taught me how to pick locks and eventually crack safes. I remember our first job. The back door of the lumber company office wasn't even locked and after we sized things up at the safe, I pulled the handle and the safe wasn't even locked." Albert chuckled, picked up his cigarette and took a long drag. "Often wonder what a person would be doing if they were raised differently? I've been pondering that over the years. You're not cut out for this life, Jimmy. It's not too late to straighten out and find gainful employment. Who knows, even settle down and raise a family."

Jimmy didn't tell Albert that's exactly what he was going to do when he sold the gold.

He finished his beer, ordered one for Albert, bid farewell and headed across the street to the Dominion Café. A plate of chicken fried rice might get him out of the funk he was in.

The early afternoon sun streamed though the big front window, bounced off the Formica-covered tables, and showed particles of dust and cigarette smoke drifting down.

Jimmy sat in a booth and lit a cigarette, put two nickels in the jukebox and chose a couple of country songs. He looked up and there was Ginger. Her white uniform and sensible shoes gave her an appearance of an innocent young thing. Maybe she was, as far as he knew.

"Hey, Ginger. When did you start working here?"

"Last week."

"How do you like it?"

"The tips are good and the hours are okay. It's mostly regulars who eat here. Single guys from the factories and kids stopping for hamburgers and cokes, but gets kind of wild after the bars close though." She took an order from the next booth, then his.

She brought his order, took a peek over at the owner standing behind the cash register, and sat down across from him. "How about meeting me in the Marigold at two when my shift ends? I need some answers: where in the hell is Ray? I don't know what to do. We had so many plans for the future. We were going to be rich and head west."

"Sure, whatever I can do to help."

Jimmy finished his raisin pie and coffee, and then walked across the street to the Marigold Tavern. It was a small homey place; mostly guys having a few drinks after work, then home to their wife and kids. There was a different atmosphere than at the Temple Tavern down the street.

He drank beer and listened to the ballgame, marked the play in the score boxes on the blackboard, while he waited for her. Ginger poked her head in from the ladies and escort room and waved. He finished his beer then walked in and over to her table.

"I'm tired, been working since six," Ginger said.

Jimmy pulled out a chair, sat down and beckoned to the waiter for two glasses of draft beer.

"I've seen you around with Ray a few times. How did you meet him?"

"My girlfriend and I were hitchhiking to work. We both worked behind the counter at Kresge's. This brand new car stopped and we got in. There was Ray. He was so good looking and a big tease. He was a real gentleman though, not like some of the idiots who come on to you. He asked me to go to a movie and I said yes." She looked at Jimmy and smiled. "I really fell for him."

She went on about Ray. Born and raised in Toronto, his father was a big wheel in the investment business and his mother quite the society lady. Ray took her to visit them. Biggest house she ever saw. Looked like one of those houses you see in the movies. Three stories high and a balcony almost across the whole second floor. Large windows with small panes encased in lead frames. A large foyer at the entrance with a marble floor led her into a parlor the size of a tennis court. As Ginger stood here looking up the curved staircase leading to the massive chandelier in the upper area it made her realize the different world she came from. If she played her cards right this could be her future. Now all those hopes and dreams might be gone. Ray even went to Upper Canada College. He didn't stay very long; education wasn't his cup of tea.

Jimmy sipped at his beer, sat back and listened. He and Ray had shared a lot but not that much of the personal stuff.

"I don't know where he is," Jimmy lied. "Any idea on what plans he had?"

"Sometimes he'd tell me some tall tales, so I didn't know what to believe. He said he had a big deal in the works after a trip to Northern Ontario. Then we would be on easy street, buy a ranch and raise cattle. He told me he always wanted to be a cowboy like the ones he saw, in the movies, when he was a kid.

Well that's Ray all right, with all his crazy dreams. Jimmy told Ginger just to hang tight. Things started to get a little clearer. Now, if you put two and two together, you come up with a pretty good idea just what Ray had in mind. His former partner had planned to screw him out of his share. It made Jimmy angry but it hurt just the same. Where's all that honor among thieves bullshit everyone talks about. Maybe it just happened in the movies.

After too much beer, Jimmy walked her home. She lived with her parents just two blocks over on Cadillac St. Hope her father was still at work, for her sake and his. Some of these old-timers would kick the shit out of you if they thought you're messing with their daughters.

He walked over to the bus stop and caught the Crosstown bus to his rooming house.

CHAPTER 8

"You're one hot chick, sweetheart," Riley said, in a slurred voice. "What's your name?"

"Hi handsome. It's Cheri."

"I'm Riley. Can I buy you a drink?"

Clover, aka Cheri, working undercover for the first time, winced and almost slugged him. This was Bogart's idea, not hers, but sometimes you have to take it and get on with the job. If anyone knew anything about Ray's problems, it would be Riley.

"Sure. I'll have a pink lady."

She had spotted Riley sitting at the bar by himself and walked over and sat on the stool beside him.

The Temple was packed with mostly factory workers, their wives, girlfriends, or both, prostitutes, guys on the make, lonely old-timers trying to forget. These were the men and women who busted their ass all week scratching out a living, most of them going to church and raising children. This was Friday night, a time to let loose for a few hours. The music from the stage was hot and heavy. Clover enjoyed the fiddle music; reminded her of the Scottish reels and jigs she square danced, waltzed and listened to at home.

"You and I can make sweet music together, Cheri."

"Why not. You're one cool dude," she managed to say. He wasn't all that good looking, kind of swarthy but had that dangerous look some women find attractive. He looked better than the photograph Bogart had given her to identify him. All Clover wanted was information.

Her cowboy boots hurt like hell and the tight leather skirt wasn't all that comfortable. The walk on the wild side was kind of intriguing though, and overall, she felt good. She kind of smiled inside, thinking about her parents' reaction if they could see her now.

She'd nursed her drink. She couldn't let her guard down; these were dangerous outlaws she was dealing with.

For some reason or other thoughts of Jimmy kept entering her mind. He was far from being a lady-killer, but had that certain something that made the ladies feel secure and cared for. He was tall and gangly with a shock of almost unmanageable black hair, full lips and high cheekbones. He reminded her of her father. There was sadness about Jimmy; his eyes were dark pools where she thought she could see his soul.

"Listen, Riley, I'm used to the best. You probably couldn't afford me." Clover said while laughing at her new name. It fit her slight Métis accent.

"I've got connections, sweetheart. Nothing goes on around town that I don't know about, and I've got my hand in quite a few ventures."

"OK, Mr. Smarty, what happened to that guy who disappeared last week? It's been in the newspaper and on the radio almost every day."

"Well, if they did a little digging in the bush they might find him," he said, giving her that smartass look that made her feel cheap.

"There's bush all over the place, where in hell would a person start?"

"Who knows, maybe around a golf course?" He leaned over and gave her a slobbering kiss on the cheek. She really felt like slugging him as hard as she could; but kept her composure, she was getting somewhere. She had him wrapped around her little finger.

The waiter brought Riley another double shot of rye and a beer. He swayed on the stool and tried to keep from falling off. He didn't notice when Clover slowly backed away, turned and walked out the door.

There was a sense of relief when she jumped into her car. She didn't care for this world she had emerged from.

She imagined her life at home, helping her mother in the kitchen, cleaning the barn, and riding on horseback over the low hills and across the grassy plains. It gave her a sense of happiness and contentment. But that was not her future: taking over the farm, picking some fine young man to marry and raise kids. What was her future? At thirty-one it was time to make a choice. Maybe she would go to teachers' college. The world of literature and art appealed to her. Even in this man's world she wanted to give it a shot.

Her roommate, Dolly, was just home from a date when Clover arrived at their apartment, a combination parlor and kitchen, with two bedrooms on the second floor of a duplex.

"That jackass so-called boyfriend of mine made another pass at me when we sat in the movie. I could have slugged him," Dolly said as she lit a cigarette. "The dumb ass must have known it was full of people." She put the kettle on to boil and took a box of tea out of a cupboard.

Dolly was kind of plump with a petulant mouth, eyes as big as saucers and tight curly blonde hair. "Where in hell were you in that getup? You look like a two-dollar whore. Those cowboy boots must hurt like hell!"

Clover laughed, "It's a long story, I'll tell you about it tomorrow. I've had a few drinks, and right now, all I want to do is take a hot bath and go to bed."

CHAPTER 9

Jimmy slowly rose from his bed and glanced at the clock; it was six thirty. He stumbled over to the ringing phone. In his world everyone is either still up from the night before or asleep at this time of day. Jumpier than a one-trick acrobat on stilts, a slight hangover and not fully awake, he picked up the phone and politely said hello.

"Jimmy?"

"Jesus, Albert, do you know what time it is?"

"Sorry Jimmy, I didn't think this could wait. Meet me at the Dominion Café in an hour," and hung up.

His stomach was tied in knots as he reached into a hamper for a shirt he'd only worn for a day and dress pants that still had a crease. Christ, this was Albert Arcand, harder than steel and tough as nails; I guess you could call him our hero. He asked no quarter and gave none. Once a friend he was a friend for life. This had to be important.

Jimmy shivered in his light jacket when he left the rooming house and caught the bus for the thirty-minute ride to the restaurant.

"What'll you have for breakfast?" asked Albert when Jimmy walked in and over to his table.

"The breakfast of champions: two fried eggs and a bottle of beer."

"Good to see you still have your sense of humor. I just ordered us bacon, eggs, toast and coffee."

Jimmy could hardly sit still, and thought he'd jump out of his skin waiting, but he knew Albert wouldn't be rushed. Think all that jail time gave him more patience than that guy in the bible, whatever in hell his name was.

"Jimmy, going by the talk around town you're involved with the gold robbery."

"Damned if I know why they think that." Maybe there's something to the intuition one con can detect from another. Maybe it's that scared and lonely feeling we get at times.

"Jesus, Albert, you're putting me in a tough spot."

"I'm not asking for myself. I don't want to know. But if you are, you got to act soon. You're not talking about the usual two-bit thieves here, Jimmy, some big time mobsters are asking around.

"How in hell would they know about it?"

"Because Riley had big ears, that's why, and who knows what Ray told him."

"Just for the hell of it, let's just say I had the gold. What do you think I should do?"

" Find someone you trust who knows something about the financial world and sell it."

"What about you?"

"I can pick any lock in the world and open any safe, but when it comes to wheeling and dealing, I'm not your man."

Jimmy thought for a minute, than looked at Albert. He trusted him. "Yeah, I have the gold."

"Well you better damn well leave town and try to sell it. They'll be closing in on you."

Jimmy felt his face flush and a vague feeling of apprehension spread over his body. He didn't want this shit. He was quite content sitting in a tavern, eating kielbasa and drinking beer with a few buddies, joking, teasing and bullshitting. Now he was hanging on a tree branch, his ass over a bunch of snapping alligators in a river below.

"Ray had the connections to sell it, so he said anyway. I haven't got a clue."

"Well, about fifteen or so years ago, I was serving time with a guy from Timmins. If my memory serves me correctly, he had some high grade gold he obtained by illegal means and sold it to a bank in Santa Fe."

"What was he doing in jail?" Jimmy asked.

"Oh the dumb bastard started spending the money like it was going out of style and the law was soon on his ass." Albert shook his head and laughed.

"Here you are, gentlemen," the waitress said and set down their breakfast.

"Thank you, Thelma," Albert said. "How's the family?"

"Could be worse. Could be better if my big lug of a husband got a job."

"They seem to be hiring all the young guys these days but I hear Ford's going to hire shortly," Jimmy said.

Thelma shrugged her shoulders, "I sure hope so," and walked away.

Jimmy finished eating, got up and put fifty cents on the table. "Have a beer and a shot when the Temple opens. Thanks for the tip and the breakfast." He shook Albert's hand and said goodbye, not knowing this was the last time he would ever talk to him.

"I have a little dough saved up. If I can help, you just have to ask," Albert said as he sipped on his coffee.

"Thanks, pal."

The bus windows were fogging up and raindrops were running down racing to the bottom, through the reflections of the streetlights as he travelled across town to his room. He looked at his face in the glass. Who is this guy? He was a dumb thief trying to sell a small fortune in gold and stay alive. He was just one step ahead of disaster: his stomach in knots and his head aching.

He got off the bus, stood, with his eyes searching for any sign of life. A car was parked opposite his rooming house. He approached the car with his heart pounding and his stomach in knots, walked past and glanced in the car window. The occupants were a couple of teenagers holding on to each other. He hurried to his room.

Jimmy opened a bottle of beer, walked over to the window, pushed aside the flimsy curtains, and watched the falling rain.

He was a sitting duck, he knew what he had to do; all it took was trust. He went to the icebox for a piece of sausage and another beer, polished them off and went to bed.

The sound of people arguing coming through the thin walls from the next room woke him up. The two guys who lived there were okay when they were sober but fought like hell when they were drunk. He got up out of bed in the darkness and walked to the window. The streetlights shone on the wet pavement and the rain pelted down. He sat on his bed and lit up a smoke. The only light was from the red glow of the cigarette. He went to the icebox for a beer, but there was none left. He put out his cigarette; lay on the bed, listening to the ticking clock until he finally fell asleep.

He awoke with a start, sat up remembering the recurring dream of a runaway train, speeding faster and faster, and he was on it.

The coffee was bubbling in the glass top of the pot and two pieces of bread were browning in the toaster. Why did Ray get himself killed? He should have known better. He'd know how to sell the gold.

Jimmy made a decision. He looked up the number in the phone book and called.

"Hello,"

"Hello Clover, this is Jimmy."

"Good morning. You're up early."

I want to see you. I think you know what it's about." He felt relieved for the first time in weeks. "Can you meet me in the bistro, at the corner of Ouellette and Erie, about two? The noonday crowd should be finished and hopefully we can talk with a bit of privacy."

"Okay, but don't forget, Jimmy, we can't turn back."

Guess she knew what he was calling about. His shoulders relaxed and the tightness in his chest was replaced by a feeling of exhilaration. For the first time since Ray's death he didn't feel alone. He lay on the bed and slept.

When Jimmy arrived at the eatery he spotted Clover sitting at a table over by a window. The place was empty except for this older guy at the table two over from them, trying to impress a young thing sitting with him; she looked about eighteen. They were eating mussels, salad and drinking wine. He was going on about his work in the music industry and his influence in the recording part of it. Clover leaned over with a smile and whispered, "What's your take on the attempt at seduction going on?"

"I think she's a young singer looking for a break. Who knows maybe it's the other way around."

"Oh no! I can spot these guys a mile away and she's not falling for it. When I glanced at her I'm sure she rolled her eyes."

The waiter brought their coffee and crème brulée.

"Okay, Jimmy, let's hear it," Clover said in a low voice.

" Just say I might have the gold."

"Dammit, lets get off on the right track. This is business, and if you want my help, be honest with me or get someone else. Lets start by you telling the truth. Where is it?"

Jimmy hesitated, looked at the ceiling, pressed his lips together and glanced at Clover. "It's buried at my cottage in Wishart Falls."

"I have to know who all is involved and has a share in the action."

'My buddy Frenchie, who works at a mining company."

"What did he have to do with it?"

"He and I were shooting the breeze, in the Maple Leaf Tavern in Timmins a few years ago, when I was up there, while visiting my mother in Wishart Falls." Jimmy lit a cigarette. It eased the pressure; who in hell can he trust? He had made the commitment so guess it doesn't matter anymore. "Frenchie was the shipping supervisor for the mining company, it was his job to make arrangements for shipping the gold to the Canadian Mint in Ottawa."

Jimmy ordered more coffee and continued. "The more beer we drank the more we talked about stealing the damn stuff. Nothing more happened until later when Ray and I were in Guelph Reformatory. I remember we were walking in the yard and I mentioned it to him. Things were put on ice until this past winter when we were released and were on what you could call at loose ends."

"You and Ray were the only ones who knew where the gold is?" Clover asked.

"Yeah, and he didn't know how to get to it."

"Okay, good."

"I called Frenchie. He was anxious to get in on it. The gold was shipped by railroad. His brother happened to be the night telegraph operator on duty in North Bay where the shipments are transferred from one train to the other. That's where the heist would take place. He called and told me when the gold was going to leave Timmins. That set things in motion and everything went like clockwork."

"What was in it for him?" Clover asked.

"Twenty percent, and he would settle with his brother."

"Now, that wasn't so hard. We just have to dig up the gold and sell it," Clover said.

" I got a tip. We may have to take a trip to Santa Fe," Jimmy said.

"Tell me about it."

"An American bank might buy it. It's been done before."

She raised her eyes. "Why not here?"

"It's too close to home."

"Okay. I'll make some calls," Clover said.

"Whatever you say."

'Okay, We're going to need money. I've got close to a thousand. How much do you have?" Clover said.

"I haven't got a hell of a lot, maybe a couple of hundred."

Clover coughed and her eyes watered. She waved the smoke away from her eyes.

"When did you start smoking again? I thought you we're going to quit."

"I'm trying,'" Jimmy said and butted out the cigarette in the ashtray.

Jimmy helped her put her jacket on and they left.

Jimmy was humming along with the song on the radio and tapping his hands on the dashboard, while she drove him home.

"I'll pick you up in the morning, Jimmy, around six. In the meantime, stay in."

He left the car, turned, waved and walked to his rooming house.

CHAPTER 10

Jimmy was grinning, and walked in a circle on the sidewalk, with his arms spread out. "I'm flying, baby," he shouted at Clover when she drove up in the early morning.

Clover rolled down the window and said, "We'll I'm not. Get in."

Jimmy opened the rumble seat, swung his suitcase in a circle and set it down beside Clover's. He sat in the car, leaned over and kissed Clover on the cheek.

"Jimmy, behave yourself. I'm not in the mood for any of your nonsense."

"This is the happiest day of my life."

"I was awake half the night, trying to figure why I agreed to this."

"It's kind of late now, sweetheart. Besides, you won't regret it. I'm going to make you the happiest woman in the world.

"That worries me too. I'm thinking of my family. What would they think of me if they knew."

Their heads jerked back when she drove off. Jimmy looked at her and grinned.

They headed up Highway 2 in her Ford coupe. The tinny sound of country music, from the radio, blasted away. The sun shone, and the sky was bluer than Daisy Mae's eyes in Jimmy's favorite comic strip.

This was going to be a fast trip: dig up the gold, visit his mother, and get the hell back where Clover could make arrangements to sell their treasure. He just hoped Clover's old coupe didn't break down.

"What are you going to tell your mother, Jimmy?"

"I don't know. I expect to be away a long time and want to say goodbye. I'll try to tell her how sorry I am to have disappointed her over the years. She and Dad had high hopes for me but I let them down."

"You can still make it up."

"It all hinges on the gold."

"Some things are more important, Jimmy. Just keep that in mind."

He didn't say anything. Why rock the boat and it wouldn't do any good anyway.

They were just past London when Clover pulled the car over to the side of the road.

"What are you stopping for?" Jimmy asked, waking up and looking around.

"I think we have a slow leak. The car seems to be lower, in front, on your side."

"I'll have a look." Jimmy got out, "Yeah, you have a flat." He walked back, opened the rumble seat and took out the spare tire and jack. "Hope your spare has enough air in it." He quickly jacked up the side of the car and changed the tire.

"You're so good at this kind of stuff, Jimmy."

Well at least I'm good at something, he thought. It was nice to hear anyway.

Jimmy took over the driving, for the short distance to Brantford, and dropped the tire off at the first gas station they came too. He saw a hand painted sign, on a board that was nailed to the side of an old building across the street that spelled RESTAURANT.

" Let's eat while they fix it. I'm hungry as hell."

"It doesn't look all that clean to me," Clover said.

"We can't be fussy," Jimmy said as they looked through the dirty windows. "It's the only one around."

The smell of freshly baked bread and coffee that greeted them when he opened the door was inviting and the open kitchen looked clean. Two teenage boys occupied a table and were drinking pop. An elderly lady dressed to the nines, sat at another sipping on a cup of tea and eating a biscuit. She smiled at Jimmy and Clover.

They sat in a booth, Jimmy put a quarter in the jukebox and picked five songs, two by Theresa Brewer, three by Judy Collins and started humming to the music. The waitress, except for a crooked tooth, wasn't all that bad to look at. She smiled at him as she set down their order of roast beef sandwiches, apple pie and coffee. The food was good.

Clover was a knockout with her pink pedal pushers and a white shirt with the two top buttons undone. Jimmy reached across and took her hand. She smiled.

Soon the gold would be in his possession. It looked like better days ahead.

The tire was fixed and changed with the spare when they returned to the garage. Jimmy paid the dollar charge and put the spare in the rumble seat. He noticed Clover had moved over to the passenger seat. He jumped in and slowly maneuvered the car into the traffic.

He wanted to see his mother again. The only problem was it would lead to recriminations and hard feelings. He'd been away for a while; he couldn't put it off much longer.

Jimmy liked driving and as the miles went by, thoughts of his life at home brought a feeling of loneliness and apprehension. He hadn't fit in. Everything seemed boring and uninspiring. His only real friend was Audrey. They wanted the same thing. Get out of town and head for the bright lights. Well, they did. Audrey ended up as a taxi dancer and waitress and he became a criminal. He now had a fortune in gold and Clover. Jesus, he couldn't fuck that up.

"Wake up, sweetheart. This is the start of a new life," he said as they drove down the dusty street to the store.

"Oh, I was dreaming. You woke me up before it was over."

"What did you dream about?"

"We were flying in an airplane going straight up into the clouds. Then somehow or other you were falling out of the window."

"That's it?"

"Yeah, that's when you woke me up." Clover straightened up, turned the rearview mirror to her face and put on fresh lipstick. "We were old, but we still looked the same. She put her hand on Jimmy's knee. "Let's do this Jimmy. It'll all work out."

"Jimmy, oh my god, Jimmy." was all his mother could say as she sobbed uncontrollably when they entered the store.

Tears were running down Jimmy's cheeks while he hugged her.

"You should have phoned," his mother said wiping her tears with the corner of her smock.

"Ma, this is my friend Clover Spence, we're in business together and I thought you would like to meet her," he said with a quavering voice as he wiped his tears away with the back of his hand.

She smiled and embraced Clover. "So nice to meet you."

"I've heard a great deal about you, Mrs. Delaney. Your son's very proud of you."

"I'm sorry to say, I'm not proud of his behavior. I don't think his father or I understood the boy. He was different. We worked six days a week in the store and his father spent a great deal of time down in the dumps. Maybe we should have tried harder."

"I wasn't different, Ma. I was looking for excitement that I couldn't find here. Then when I did find it, I went down the wrong path."

"Let bygones be bygones," his mother said, as she took off her smock and put on her apron.

Yeah, I'm sure she will, Jimmy thought.

Jimmy waited on a few customers while his mother and Clover cooked supper and chatted in the kitchen.

The aroma of a beef roast filled the room as they sat down to eat. Mashed potatoes, thick dark-brown gravy, carrots and canned peaches made Jimmy feel that he had finally came home.

"This is the happiest I've been for a long time," Mrs. Delaney said. It's been my dream. Only thing to make it perfect would be a child sitting with us."

"One thing at a time, Ma."

"I'm not getting any younger. I want to be a grandmother before I die."

"Who knows what the future holds?" Clover said. "You must be tired, Mrs. Delaney. Jimmy and I'll clean up."

"That's so nice of you, Clover." Mrs. Delaney walked into the parlor, sat on her rocking chair and turned on the radio.

"It's nice to have a man helping with the dishes," Clover said.

"My dad never did them," Jimmy said.

"Mine neither. My mother said it was women's work."

"Your mother was a smart lady."

Clover reached into the soapy water and flicked it at him. Jimmy stepped behind her, put his arms around her, and kissed her behind the ear.

"Jimmy, stop that," she whispered and leaned back closer to him. They laughed.

"We're all done now, Ma. We're going to the cottage, and get settled in."

"What did you say, son?" his mother said turning down the radio.

"We're leaving for the cottage now. We need a couple of days to relax, I'm sure there's work for us to do around the store."

"Just enjoy yourselves. I have a handyman. He's not very good but he does get the job done."

The sun was disappearing beyond the horizon and the pine trees cast long shadows across the road.

"Your mother is a nice lady and I'm very happy to have met her," Clover said when she entered the car.

"She sure is happy. She likes you, Clover."

"I like her. She needs you, Jimmy."

"Yes, I know."

Clover snuggled up beside him and rested her head on his shoulder. "We can dig up the gold in the morning when there's daylight."

"Let's dig it up now."

"Jimmy, its been buried for months, another day won't make any difference." Besides it's dark."

They backed out of the driveway and drove the two-miles to the cottage. A mist covered the long winding road through the birch and poplar forest as they approached the lake; it gave Jimmy an eerie feeling. They entered a completely different world. The tall swaying pine trees surrounded a small cottage with batten board siding, low-pitched roof, and a rain barrel at the corner of the front porch. The light from the moon shimmered on the rippling water, ghostlike through the fog.

The sense of enchantment cast a spell when they opened the door and entered. The mesmerized Jimmy stood quietly as Clover approached and embraced him.

They made love as the light of the moon streamed through the open window and bounced in rhythm off the walls and reflected off the dresser mirror. The sounds of rustling leaves, the swooping sounds of bats and the distant wailing of a train whistle made it surreal. Jimmy was engulfed in a sense of fulfillment he had never experienced before.

The sun was just over the horizon when Jimmy awoke. He looked over at the sleeping Clover and gently shook her shoulder. "It's time, sweetheart." He rose from the bed and quickly dressed.

Clover sat up, her eyes opened wide, "Oh. Jimmy, this is it." She reached for her dress on the chair and pulled it over her head. "I'm a nervous wreck."

"I can't wait. Let's dig."

Jimmy walked to the shed, unlocked the door and took out a shovel. Clover followed him behind the outhouse.

"Oh no!" he shouted looking at the gaping holes in the ground. "It's gone! The gold is gone." He threw the shovel into the trees and kicked at the piles of dirt.

"Are you sure this is where you hid it?"

"Dammit, Clover, of course it is. Do you think I'd forget something like that? It took me an hour to dig a hole through the frozen ground."

"You may have buried it somewhere else, it was during the night."

Jimmy sat down on a nearby stump and shouted. "It was here. The goddamn gold is gone." He looked up and saw the tears in Clover's eyes.

He covered his face with his hands and sobbed. "It's just that our future's gone."

"I don't understand, Jimmy. Who do you think would know where the gold was hidden?"

"Ray was with me, but it was pitch black, he was holding the flashlight and didn't know where the cabin was and how to get here." Jimmy rose and walked down to the lake with Clover following him. He sat on a log. "All my hopes and dreams are gone."

"Get a grip, Jimmy. Crying won't do any good. Let's stay for one more day then go back to Windsor."

Jimmy knew he had to for his mother's sake and what the hell difference did it make? It was all over.

"Let's go to your mother's for breakfast. We still have to eat."

"I don't want to go," he walked back up to the cottage, went into the bedroom, shut the door and sat on the bed.

"It isn't the end of the world, we'll get through this. You can get a job and support us while I go to teachers college," she hollered at the closed door.

Jimmy didn't answer.

"You have to, please do it for me." He didn't answer."

Finally Jimmy came out of the bedroom and walked to the sink, picked up the dipper, put water in the wash basin, and washed his face. He looked out the window and saw Clover sitting on a stump looking out into the lake. He still had her, she was more important to him than the gold. He walked down to her, took her hands and raised her up and hugged her. Clover cried softly.

"I was finally doing something, making a success out of my life for the first time, Jimmy said. "It hurts, Clover, it hurts."

Clover looked up at him, her eyes opened wide. "We're together, what else do we need?"

Jimmy attempted a smile.

"Straighten up, Jimmy, you don't want your mother to see you like this."

"I don't really care anymore."

"Please."

Jimmy let Clover take his hand and lead him to the car. She drove to his mother's.

"Good morning, Mrs. Delaney," Clover said and gave her a peck on the cheek.

"Please, just call me Anne."

Jimmy walked to the kitchen table and sat down. He looked at his mother. He had never seen her beaming like this. It lasted until she looked at him.

"What are you mooning about? You're acting like your father."

Jimmy didn't say anything. Maybe his father had plans too. Maybe he had dreams of a different life.

"Please light a fire, Jimmy," his mother said.

Jimmy got up and walked to the cook stove, opened the lid and put in a crumpled piece of newspaper, kindling wood and lit it.

"Maybe a big breakfast of ham and eggs will cheer you up," his mother said and picked up the cast iron fry pan hanging on a nail beside the stove.

It'll take a hell of a lot more than that, Jimmy thought. "I'll be okay, Ma."

"I know you will. You're lucky to have someone like Clover with you."

"We take care of each other, Mrs. Delaney."

"I'm going to quit worrying about that boy, Now, Jimmy, you listen to Clover."

"Aw, Ma. I'm a grown man." He sat with an elbow on the table and toyed with the ham and finally ate half of an egg.

"Jimmy suggested we work around the store today, Anne. We need the exercise," Clover said as she rose from the table. "That was a great breakfast."

"Thanks, Clover."

Weeds grew around the sparse phlox and pansy plants trying to survive, planted in the sandy soil, in front of the store. The front lawn of mostly plantain and twitch grass seemed to cling to the raised earth with defiance. It was like the people who lived on this hard land. The towns and villages that thrived until the trees were all cut down or the minerals all taken out of the ground, then they packed up and moved to the next one. Their only help was from their faith and each other. They built their homes, raised their children, buried their dead and carried on.

Jimmy looked at Clover, down on her knees, pulling weeds. He was one lucky bastard. He didn't have the gold but something more precious. He leaned the rake against the wall and walked over to her. "I'm sorry about this morning, sweetheart." He put his arms under hers and swung her around.

"Jimmy put me down, what will your mother think? It's damn near noon, let's go for a swim," she said wiping the sweat from her face. "Your mother might want to come."

"I doubt it, but I'll ask her."

Jimmy stuck his head in the store, "Ma, Clover and I are going to the cottage, you coming?

"I can't. I have to mind the store. But, thanks anyway. You did enough work for today.

"Why don't you go out tonight and maybe run into some of your old friends? It might cheer you up." She quickly got back to reading *True Confessions*.

The rising clouds of sand that followed the car ahead limited their visibility and slowed them down. Jimmy waved back at three boys turning off to a road into the bush, with slingshots in their hands. It seemed like yesterday he was doing the same thing. He wondered what their future held.

They exited the car; Jimmy walked to the porch, sat and stared out at the lake. Clover went into the cottage. He heard the door slam and turned to see Clover running to the lake with nothing on but her beaded necklace and a grin. He jumped up and ran after her tearing off his shirt and stumbling while pulling his pants off. She squealed as he chased her into the deep water. After the ten-minute swim they ran back up the hill and through the door into the bedroom. Jimmy caressed her, pulled the sheets down and followed her into bed.

A clap of thunder woke Jimmy. He glanced over at the sleeping Clover, got up, dressed, walked outside and lit a cigarette. He went towards the outhouse; picked up the shovel he had thrown and covered the holes. His face became red and his throat constricted as thoughts of what might have been came flooding back. He couldn't help it.

The ladies and escort section of the Bissonettes Hotel was a change from the noisy and busy Temple Tavern back in Windsor. A dozen or so patrons sat around four of the twelve tables, drinking beer. Voices droned on and laughter was sometimes heard. A waiter sitting behind the counter waited for someone to order.

Like most of these small villages, the young people left town at the first opportunity. Jimmy didn't know a damn soul.

The beer was cold and refreshing. The more he drank the more he thought of the loss. "I'm leaving this town and not coming back," he said.

"Whatever you say. It's nine o'clock, let's go home," Clover said.

"I don't want to go."

"Well, I am. Give me the keys. I'm going."

Jimmy gave her the keys, rose unsteadily and followed her out.

"You'll feel better about things after a good night's sleep. We'll stop at your mother's for breakfast, than drive to Windsor. Please try and look happy for your mother's sake."

"Sure, I'll be happy old Jimmy."

"You give me a pain sometimes. We'll get through this together."

Jimmy walked over to the bed and lay on the covers. He glanced at Clover sitting on a rocking chair staring at the waning moon, closed his eyes and fell asleep.

The rain was sweeping across the lake and the light green leaves forming on the poplar and birch trees were shaking in the early morning light. Jimmy and Clover ran to the car. Jimmy sat glassy eyed, with his head down as Clover drove to the store.

"All is not lost, Jimmy," Clover said. "The gold's still around somewhere."

Jimmy didn't answer.

Jimmy sat and watched Clover set the table and his mother ladle out the pancake mixture into a fry pan. The aroma of bacon sizzling in another pan filled the kitchen.

Jimmy's eyes watered as he studied his mother pouring tea. There was a slight tremor in her hands and she seemed lost in the dress that covered her stooped frame.

"I'm going to come home more often, Ma."

"That would be so wonderful. Maybe I can visit you and Clover when you settle down."

"Oh, yes," Clover said. "I hope it's soon, and you can stay as long as you want."

"It would be great to get away from here for a month or so during the cold winters."

Jimmy frowned and looked at Clover, "Let's eat breakfast and get moving."

Jimmy slowly drove away. He tooted the horn and they both waved at his smiling mother.

CHAPTER 11

The spindly trees planted along the street were too far apart to keep the hot sun from Jimmy's back as he walked the seven blocks to Bogart's office. What news did he have? The ten o'clock call woke him up from a troubled sleep. Who stole the gold bricks he stashed? Where's the gold now? So much for his rosy future, he could have been set for life. Sixty grand; he wouldn't earn that much if he worked in a factory for twenty years or ran his mother's store.

Jimmy's dreams of a life with Clover might be over. He didn't have big plans – no flights to Havana to party, raise hell, drink and carouse for the rest of his days. He'd be happy with a new fedora, a better suit and a better brand of whiskey on his bedside table. More importantly, maybe marry Clover and raise a family and buy a house in the new suburbs being built. To have his mother say just once, Jimmy, I'm proud of you. It would make it all worthwhile. Thinking of the opportunities when they had sold the gold added to his misery. All those years trying to grab the golden ring were never as close. Hopefully, seeing Clover again would help his troubled mind.

The door to Bogart's office was ajar when Jimmy arrived. Bogart was in his usual position, tilted back on his chair with his feet on the desk, talking on the phone. Looked like he bought a new suit; double breasted and gabardine. Business must be picking up. Clover, dressed in a red silk blouse, black skirt, raven black hair in a ponytail, bright red lipstick, and a hint of rouge on her cheeks raised his spirits, but even as she gave him this enticing smile, he thought again of what he may have lost.

"Got some news for you, Jimmy," Bogart said, as he sat upright in his chair and hung up the phone. "The police, acting on an anonymous tip, with some new information, found Ray's body buried in a shallow grave in the woods by the Little River Golf Course. The autopsy report showed he was shot through the chest at close range with a .22 pistol. The strange thing is they found the gun on the floor in his apartment."

Jimmy's heart sank. Ray had betrayed him, but he still thought of him as a brother. More than that it was Ray that made his life an adventure: his schemes, his dreams, chatter and the parties. Even the jail time was dramatic at times. Even those in the higher hierarchy, bank robbers and killers, liked him. He brought out the best in everyone. It all brought Jimmy bittersweet memories. They were buddies: double dating, drinking and carousing.

"Maybe it was a suicide?" Jimmy said.

"No, the gun was six feet from the body." Bogart leaned back in his chair and continued, "My connections within the police department tell me they knew all about Ray holding back betting slips, which of course would put him in deep trouble with the mob. The only fly in the ointment is those bastards wouldn't use a small caliber pistol, more likely a 9-millimeter or a .45 and they wouldn't have left it at the scene. The cops are going to be on your ass, Jimmy. Stay out of trouble."

Now, that's something he didn't have to tell him. All Jimmy wanted to do was stay out of trouble and find a better job than running the gambling joint.

"We just have to wait this out, Jimmy," Bogart said, and then turned to Clover. "Why don't you take him for a coffee and a slab of pie to ease his troubled mind?" Bogart stood up. "I'm going upstairs to see if mother will make coffee. Oh, another thing, regarding the objects you brought in from Ray's apartment. I think the train tickets for Vancouver was for a getaway. Looks like a couple of people were going to skip town."

"We have the key with the number 359 stamped on it too," said Clover.

"Thanks, Bogart," Jimmy said.

"Let's go, big guy," she said, put on lipstick and teased her hair.

The coffee shop, just past the corner on Mill Street, had a counter and about ten stools. It was deserted. Jimmy only wanted coffee. When Clover took his hand, giving it a light squeeze, his spirits rose and the sky looked a lighter blue through the smeared window. As the smoke curled up from his cigarette sitting in the ashtray, his mind wondered back to those happy days when he thought the gold was safely hidden. "Clover, do you think we have a future together?"

"Who knows, Jimmy, I'm here, aren't I?" She finished her banana split, picked up her purse and put a dollar on the table. "The spirits will let me know."

What in hell did that mean? She turned to see if anyone was looking, then quickly pulled him towards her by the lapels of his jacket. She slowly moistened her lips, partly opened her mouth and kissed him.

"I have to get back to work," she said.

Jimmy escorted Clover back to the office and with his head still spinning from the kiss, jumped on a bus and headed over to the Temple Hotel.

The faint smell of old beer and tobacco seemed to go with the music. It brought feelings and thoughts of lost love, betrayal and hope, all wrapped up in Hank Snow's song "I'm Moving On" sung by the three musicians on the small stage.

Where was Albert? He wasn't at his usual table.

Jimmy slowly surveyed the crowd and spotted Albert in a far corner. Jimmy stopped, turned back and sat at the bar. Albert was sitting with two guys. The big one hunched over was wearing a gray hat tilted back on his head, rumpled seersucker suit covering a white t-shirt. His nose looked like it had been on the wrong end of a swinging fist a few times. The other guy looked like a Toledo pimp, all decked out in a bright blue suit, blue shirt and blue-striped tie. A black hat with a wide blue stripe completed the ensemble. He was a little guy compared to the other, but he looked twice as mean and dangerous.

Albert looked to be well into his cups. Good thing too. Otherwise, he might have noticed Jimmy from across the smoke-filled room. Jimmy would rather have a chat with Albert when he didn't have that pair of assholes on his wings.

Jimmy finished a beer and thought it might be a good time to visit Audrey. After all, she had been in love with Ray and was the first to find his body. Jimmy turned, walked into the kitchen and out the back door.

Memories came back to Jimmy. He and Ray had been friends since he moved to Windsor, after he and Audrey left that god-forsaken town of Wishart Falls and headed for the bright lights. They were searching for something missing in their lives. Guess they wanted something bigger and better, more excitement, more opportunity. Well that didn't happen.

Jimmy walked three blocks over to Audrey's apartment and knocked on the door. "How are you, Audrey?" he said when she opened the door.

Her face was pale, eyes puffy and hair uncombed. She seemed lost in the robe she was wearing.

"Come in, Jimmy."

"Thanks."

"I feel like hell. Heard about Ray on the radio. I thought he and I had a future but he threw me away. Took up with that little floozy, Ginger," she said. Her voice was bitter and her cold blue eyes looked opaque when she raised her head and looked at him.

"I'm sorry, Audrey."

"Slinging hash and dancing with a bunch of torn down bastards at the dime a dance place is my future."

"We all make mistakes," Jimmy said. "I sure as hell made my share."

"You're a great guy, Jimmy. I hope we'll always be friends."

"We will, Audrey. I haven't got much. If there's any way I can help, let me know."

"Maybe I should have listened to my parents. I plan on going home for the rest of the summer. When I think about it, they had my best interest at heart."

"Hey, let's not get carried away," he said. That made her smile, but it turned into a grimace as she kissed his cheek. "Thanks for stopping by, Jimmy."

Frankly, he was glad to get out of there. He felt bad enough about Ray. He didn't need Audrey on his mind. Problem was that going home wouldn't be better for Audrey; you can't run away from your troubles.

Sitting in his room, in his underwear, the next morning, Jimmy listened to WJR Detroit on the radio. He cut the mold off the crust of two slices of bread and made a peanut butter and jam sandwich, then put the kettle on the hotplate to boil water for tea He felt lonely and had this anxious feeling in his stomach. There was a longing he couldn't figure out. Maybe because it was Sunday morning, it bought back memories of walking down the hill to the little church with his parents. His mother would play the organ and everyone sang his favorite hymn, Abide with Me.

The phone rang and brought him out of his reverie.

"Hello?"

The sobbing was uncontrollable, than a quivering voice. "Jimmy, this is Ginger. I heard the news on the radio this morning."

"I'm sorry, Ginger."

"Oh Jimmy, I miss him so much." The sobbing was softer now. "He told me we were going to head west, live on easy street, party all day and make love all night. He was so romantic."

That was Ray: if bullshit were music he'd have the whole Grand Old Opry. "Let's hope there's better days ahead, Ginger. Did the cops call you?"

"Yes. There's something I've been holding back from you. On the last evening I spent with Ray, he mentioned a meeting the next afternoon with a mob guy named Riley to straighten out an incident that happened,"

"Did you ask what it was about?"

"Yeah, but all he said was not to worry my pretty little head about it: he had big plans. I told the cops about the meeting Ray had with this Riley guy."

"Great, Ginger," Jimmy said, breathing a sigh of relief. That gave O'Connor a new lead and would keep him off his tail for a while.

"Did Ray ever mention anything about why he had to go to Northern Ontario before you were heading west?"

Ginger hesitated, as if she was trying to remember. "No, all he said was we were going to be rich. Guess that's not going to happen, Jimmy."

"If you need any help, give me a call.

"I will."

CHAPTER 12

What in hell did Bogart want this time? Jimmy thought as stepped off the bus at the corner of Mill and Wyandotte. The call sounded kind of urgent. Jimmy had worked at the gambling den until four in the morning and hadn't slept that much when he got the call around ten.

Jimmy opened the door without knocking and ran down stairs to Bogart's office. His face looked as somber as a cat caught outside in a thunderstorm. When Bogart got up from his chair and walked over to meet him, Jimmy knew something was haywire.

"Sorry I have to break this to you, Jimmy. Our friend Albert was found in his room at the Temple Hotel with five bullets in his body."

Jimmy sat down, put his elbows on his knees and lowered his head, staring at the floor.

"He died like he lived, beholden to no one. One tough old bastard," Bogart said. Jimmy lit a cigarette and took a few long drags. His world kind of fell apart and he felt like he had been kicked in the stomach by a merry-go-round horse. He held back on the crying. Only thing that showed were a few tears. Albert was a true friend. When they served time together, he was someone to lean on and ask for advice. When a guy needed a few bucks, or wanted to go straight and needed support, he went to see Albert. He was a father figure to those of them who have been in and out of jail. Even the cops respected him. He never lied unless he had to.

"Sorry I had to break this to you, Jimmy. He had a few enemies around town but don't think they would do a thing like this. I think something is going down and it's going to get messy."

"Who in hell would do this?"

Bogart stood up and put his hands in his pockets. "He knew many dangerous people and a lot of secrets. You have to remember he lived a life of crime."

Good thing my life of crime is over, Jimmy thought.

"He made me his executor after I defended him in a murder trial a few years ago. He's left his estate to you, Jimmy."

"What! I don't want anything to do with it. I have enough worries at it is."

"Think it over, Jimmy. If you don't do it, the money will revert to the Crown. He needs a Christian burial for one thing and a party for his friends and enemies will be in order. He had about five hundred dollars in the bank and a shoebox of documents that we'll have to go through."

"Oh, Christ, This is something I have to do, there's no doubt about that. He was like an uncle to me. Yeah, OK, but I need your help."

"Come to my office tomorrow morning around nine. It'll be closed so there'll be some privacy and we can look this whole thing over," Bogart said.

"Okay, see you in the morning." Jimmy left for home and hopefully to get more sleep before work tonight. He closed the blinds and lay down.

The train was running in a circle, smoke was belching from the smokestack and he was hanging onto the grab bar on the caboose. Ray was running alongside trying to jump on. He awoke from his dream to the sound of a vacuum cleaner running somewhere in the hall. He opened a can of spaghetti, heated it up, ate, and then walked to work.

The place was full and most of the poor suckers playing stud poker were losing as usual. Jimmy felt he'd be a happy man when he could kiss this job goodbye. Running a gambling joint's a tough job. With Albert in his thoughts it was difficult putting up with all the bullshit. Guys crying the blues, cursing and lamenting about their fucked up lives gave him a pain in the ass. He wondered where that idiot Riley was. He's usually around to get on his nerves. The place cleared out around five. Jimmy walked home and went to bed.

Jimmy woke up and looked at the clock: nine. The picture of Jesus on the cross still hung crooked on the wall but he seemed to be looking at him with a more caring eye. Maybe he could see a change in him. Who knows, maybe he's growing up. He was feeling okay, but tired as hell.

He hurriedly ate half a can of cold spaghetti and a slice of bread. He was fifty feet from the bus stop when the bus pulled away. The next one came in fifteen minutes.

"Sorry I'm late, Bogart, " Jimmy said as he entered his office. "Had a late night. Friday's busy and every poor son-of-a-bitch thinks they're going to get rich."

"I know all about that," Bogart said, "Hopefully I can stay on the straight and narrow."

"They say it's a never-ending battle."

"You don't know the half of it, Jimmy."

What in hell did that mean?

"Sit at Clover's desk. This won't take all that long, and then you can go back to bed. You look like hell."

"Thanks, Bogart. I can use a coffee."

"Mother makes the coffee around here. She didn't come home last night. I think she has a boyfriend. Let's get this over with then go for breakfast."

Bogart reached in the safe, took out a shoebox with a faded blue ribbon tied around it and handed it to Jimmy. He untied it and took out six or seven papers and put them on the desk. An honorable discharge, the paper yellow and broken at the creases, from the US navy dated 1943 was on top, followed by a birth certificate from the State of Kentucky. "Jesus, he was only fifty-seven."

"Many of those old guys had a hard life," Bogart said. "When you figure the drinking and carousing and not eating properly, it's a wonder they even last that long. It sure took its toll on me."

"Jail time doesn't help either," Jimmy said.

A snapshot of a pretty young thing, wearing a skirt and sweater with a ribbon in her hair, standing by the door of a model A Ford was next. Scrolled across the back was a notation, *Will be waiting for you Al, Cathy.* Jimmy passed it to Bogart, who took a long look at it. His eyes watered and his hand shook when he passed it back, there was some kind of connection there.

Most of them left someone behind when they went off to war.

Guess when you think about it, everyone had a past that's full of regrets, sadness as well as happiness. There was a small photo of an elderly couple, the man sitting in a rocking chair and the woman standing beside him, a bankbook and black leather-covered Bible. An envelope addressed to Jimmy was the last. Damn, what in hell was this? "It's marked private," he said looking up at Bogart. He hurriedly put it in his pocket and tried to think of what to say if Bogart made a comment. Thankfully, he didn't.

"I've arranged a burial for tomorrow," Bogart said. His remains are at the Chapelle Funeral Home. There are no relatives as far as I can ascertain. Clover, you and I'll be attending. I figure we should have the sendoff next Saturday. I'll drop around to the Temple and ask Lucky if it's OK. In my books, he's the only decent hotel owner in town."

"Sounds good to me. Albert always liked a party," Jimmy said. "Hope you'll be the MC. I'm no damn good at speaking to a crowd."

"Yeah, I'll do it, Jimmy."

Jimmy fought back the tears as he walked home. Big boys don't cry, but damn, he's going to miss Albert.

The envelope from Albert was on his mind, when he walked into his room. What the hell was in it? He hurriedly tore the envelope open. Scrawled across a single page were the words, *look in train or bus station*. Damn. Albert sure made this difficult. What in hell is that supposed to mean. Jimmy sat in his room staring at the page. It didn't make any sense to him so he folded it up and stuck it in his back pocket.

Clover and Bogart were waiting when Jimmy came out of his rooming house the next morning. He jumped in the back-seat of Bogart's car, said good morning and rode in silence to the funeral home, each lost in their thoughts.

Three old gentlemen sat at the back of the room for the service. A young guy, in a suit two sizes too big for him, wearing a bowtie read a few passages from the bible. Bogart read the twenty-third psalm and Clover recited the Our Father. Jimmy, Clover and Bogart followed the funeral director's car and Albert's remains were in the hearse behind it as they left for the cemetery.

Jimmy followed the casket from the hearse, Clover held his hand to the gravesite, and Bogart walked behind them. They stood in the rain and watched four guys lower the casket into the grave on ropes.

"You were a good man, straight and true. Goodbye old friend." Jimmy said as he stared down on Albert's casket then threw a handful of sand on it.

Heat was radiating off the sidewalk and the brick walls of the Temple Tavern. It was only ten thirty when Jimmy and Clover arrived. Saturday morning had the usual hustle and bustle: women shopping, children on their way to the beach. A few men stood on the street corners trying to make sense out of it all.

"Who put the balloons up?" Clover asked.

"I asked Lucky to put them up. It would be something Albert would appreciate. He had enough sadness in his life," said Jimmy.

Clover looked prim, yet gorgeous in a small black dress with a single strand of pearls. She sat at the table, with Jimmy and Lucky, next to the stage. Extra waiters were going to be on duty, even the one who served on roller skates. The three musicians were on stage tuning up and practicing a hymn Bogart requested. The whores wouldn't be working today, keeping with the solemnity of the occasion.

The doors were opened right at twelve o'clock There must have been one hell of a lineup because the place filled in about three minutes. A roped-off section in front of the stage held most of Albert's old friends. I think every rounder in town was there. Some were dressed in fancy gabardine suits and hats. Others wore torn and battered shirts and pants and looked like they needed a drink to get through the day.

Lucky stood up and shouted, "The first round's on me!"

Then Jimmy got up, "Albert's buying for the rest of the afternoon!" The hollering and clapping was deafening.

The musicians opened with "Blue Moon of Kentucky." One of the older whores got up on stage and sang the song with a sad, quivering voice. Albert would have been proud.

"Where in hell is Bogart?" Jimmy asked Clover. "He should have been here an hour ago. He promised to do the speaking."

"I have no idea. He's been pretty dependable since he got off the sauce. Must have been something important. "You're going to have to do it, Jimmy. I know you can."

Jimmy hurried to the bar and ordered a double shot of bar rye and drank it down. He finished his beer and, feeling more comfortable, stepped up on the stage.

"Ladies and gentlemen. Welcome to the send-off for Albert Arcand. Most of us drank with him and some of us did jail time with him. He never wavered when he offered hope and help, a true and genuine friend. Many a greenhorn owes him for teaching them how to survive in the system. He'll go down in history as the best safecracker in the business."

Jimmy let the cheering go on for about a minute, than raised his hand for silence. He invited anyone with fond memories to come up and share them.

A good-looking older guy was the first speaker. His brown suit was creased and worn at the elbows. The frayed cuffs rested on shoes that were down at the heels, but he carried it all with dignity.

"Most people refer to me as Louisiana Lawson, mainly because I'm from there and Lawson's my name. I've robbed a few banks over the years but done my time. You get to know a lot about a man when sharing a jail cell. You might not believe this but he said his prayers every night. Not down on his knees, but sitting on his bed before turning in. He told me, except for picking locks and opening safes, he pretty well lived by the golden rule. His old mother would have wanted it that way. So long old friend and God bless you."

The next guy up wore a suit that must have cost him a hundred dollars. Shirt and tie with diamond cuff links made him stand apart.

"Who in the hell is that?" Clover asked Lucky.

"He's from Hamilton. Think he has ties to the Buffalo mob."

"I'm called Jake. I was a young punk when I first met Albert. Thought I was a tough guy and had no respect for anyone. I found out later that Albert talked a guy out of putting a hit on me for rubbing him the wrong way. He later gave me some walking-around money when I got out of jail. Albert, I owe you."

He received a round of applause when he left the stage and with three other suited guys went out the door.

Magnificent Millicent walked up to the stage, from a table along the wall, with a glass of beer in her hand. Her orange hair was in a big bouffant and she tottered along on high-heels, wearing a skirt and sweater, that showed why she had that nickname. "Albert was a true gentleman. He treated us with respect. I expect to meet him again in heaven. I have been elected to speak on behalf of the working girls in the area." She raised her glass to the crowd. "This is a toast to our dear friend. May he rest in peace with the Lord."

After three or four more guys took the stage and paid their respects the band started up again. When they played and sang, *There's a Gold Mine in the Sky Faraway*, Jimmy thought, hell, that's a sign. Hope that's not where his gold was. They finished up with *Abide with Me*.

" Thanks everyone for coming. It's been a wonderful afternoon and I'm sure Albert is proudly looking down on us," Jimmy said, getting off the stage for the final time.

"You were great, Jimmy," Clover said, "I knew you could do it. "

"You had more faith in me than I did. The booze helped. Where in hell is Bogart?"

"He's a big boy. I'm sure he can handle himself. My roommate's gone home to visit her family. Lets go to my place and celebrate. Who knows, you might even get lucky."

"Sure," Jimmy said, trying to look smoother than those Hollywood dandies, but damn, if this was his reward for being an MC, he was going to MC every occasion from now to his own damn memorial service.

CHAPTER 13

Bogart opened the door to a small Italian restaurant on Erie Street, with the red tablecloths covering the tables, and a pretty waitress bustling about. The smell of fresh coffee and cinnamon brought back memories of the small bistros he'd visited in Rome when on leave from the fighting.

He sat down at a table near the kitchen, lit up a cigarette, leaned back and stared out the window.

Fighting his way with the Canadian army through Sicily was tough going. Battling the elite German paratrooper divisions up the boot of Italy was tougher yet. The shrapnel in his legs still hurt at times, especially when it rained. The hospital staff could have kept them longer to recuperate but the generals needed them, they said, and rushed them back to the lines. Almost as painful and frightening were the nightmares. Drinking helped for a while, but now all he got from it was a feeling of helplessness and depression. He had to stay off the damn stuff even though he never felt whole. Every day was a battle.

"What will you have today, sir?"

Bogart jumped and his eyes opened wide as he came out of his reminiscing. The pretty waitress, with the long blond hair and gold cross on a chain around her neck, matched the description Jimmy had given him. This must be Audrey.

"Hello," he said, and ordered a western sandwich, raisin pie, and black coffee.

She was the one who'd discovered Ray's body and asked Jimmy to check him out. What else did she do or know? Did she try to set Jimmy up?

"This is a great lunch, miss. I'll be eating here more often." he said, and handed her a fifty cents tip.

"Well, thank you, sir. I'm here most days. Will be looking for you."

Bogart liked the big smile she gave him. Ten cents was about the average tip. She seemed impressed.

"My name's Bogart."

"I'm Audrey," she replied, thinking he had the look to match his moniker and might have come straight from the movie screen in Casablanca.

Bogart finished his second cup of coffee, butted out his cigarette, waved goodbye and headed to his car.

It was a long shot, but she might know this Riley character. He's the head of the local bad guys who work for the Purple Gang. Ray should have known you couldn't cross these guys. Guess Jimmy was right, Ray just didn't give a damn about anything.

He drove down Wyandotte Street and turned onto a side street trying to find a parking spot near the Temple. It took him ten minutes, and he had to park three blocks away.

He stepped out of his Packard, bent down and glanced in the side mirror to straighten his tie and pat down the little hair he had left. What in hell was he going to say about Albert? He couldn't go on about Albert's illustrious career as a safecracker, or when he shot and killed the guy he caught in bed with his wife. As he pondered this dilemma he felt a hand on his shoulder. Turning quickly, he found himself staring at a gorilla, a guy with a face only a mother could love and that would be only on payday. His mustard- colored suit was two sizes too small and his tie hung down about eight inches.

"Mr. Smithers?" the gorilla asked.

He knows me. Bogart wasn't frightened. He'd faced danger too many times, but he knew this was trouble. Before he could answer, a fist hit him on the right cheekbone and knocked him to the pavement.

"Stay away from Audrey!" The gorilla turned and strode away.

He slowly got up and stumbled back to his car, sat for a few minutes, than drove home. He certainly couldn't go to Albert's service. His head was spinning and he could taste the blood oozing over a few loosened teeth. What would his mother say?

CHAPTER 14

This damn skirt is tighter than hell, and too short for my liking, thought Clover, as she drove to the White Tavern. Working undercover was a pain and an embarrassment. Her cute-sounding handle, Cheri, didn't help even though she liked the sound of it. She hoped no one remembered her from Albert's send off. At least Riley hadn't attended, and that was the guy she was looking for. Clover hoped he was too drunk to remember their last conversation.

The room was about half-full mostly with regulars. Monday nights were pretty quiet, which made picking out Riley that much easier. She put on her game face and made her entrance count. Her low-cut blouse and the darkness between her thighs that showed as she eased herself slowly onto the bar stool, drew more than a few low whistles. She was every man's dream.

She ordered a pink lady, glanced in the mirror and slowly panned the room. Before she could so much as sip her drink there was Riley, up from his table and walking unsteadily towards her.

"Hey, Cheri," he said, as he sat on the stool beside her and tried not to fall off. "Where you been, sweetheart? I haven't seen you around lately."

Damn, I hate this part of the job. "I'm a busy girl, handsome. Guess you can say I'm enjoying life and still looking for the right guy."

"What do you say we hit some of the hot spots tonight, Cheri?"

"That'll be swell, Riley. I'd like to know more about you." That ought to get him more interested. Men always like to talk about themselves. "Maybe you're the man of my dreams. Where you from?"

"Well, I'm no Lancelot, Cheri. Had a good upbringing even though my dad left us. Just my brother, mother and I worked the farm out on the prairies."

"That's it?" she said. "You're whole life story?"

Riley shook his head and leaned close. She could smell the booze on his breath. "I'm going to tell you something, don't tell anybody."

"I won't."

He hesitated, stammered and finally spoke, "When I was in grade eight, I wrote a poem and it was published in the newspaper. It was some kind of contest and I won."

"You don't say. What was it about?'

"Hardly remember now. Something about my future and what I wanted to be."

"What did you want to be?"

"What the hell difference does it make? I'm sure not that person now. Don't ask dumb questions. I even sang in the choir. Let's go over to Pitt Street. Too damn quiet around here."

"Sure, why not. A girl has to have fun." Clover thought there were tears in Riley's eyes. For a brief moment she felt sorry for the guy.

"Call us a cab, bartender," he said, and he passed him a dollar bill.

The cab ride was a nightmare. She fought off roaming hands and his attempts to kiss her. What she'd give for a baseball bat, "Hold on there Riley, we have a long night ahead of us." She guessed he took that for a promise, as he laughed and quieted down.

A trio, playing jazz, under the soft and mellow lights that hung from the ceiling, sounded good and kept the few patrons interested. A corner of the room, with the lights low, kept it kind of private. This was her kind of place. Other than two guys quietly arguing at the next table, it had the makings of an enjoyable evening.

"I think we can make beautiful music together, Cheri."

"I'm expensive, Riley. The last guy I dated is serving time for trying to live up to my lavish tastes."

"You don't have to worry about that. I'm well connected and on the way to the top," he said, with that dumb sneer of his.

"Talk is cheap, Riley. Money buys the whiskey." One thing she'd learned over the years. When it comes to impress women,

men are dumb as hell and love to brag, especially when they were full of booze.

"Ever hear of the Purple gang?" he asked.

"All I know is that they're a Jewish gang from Detroit and have fingers reaching over here."

"They've been in business for a long time. Even Al Capone didn't go near them back in the day. They're hard bastards."

"My kind of guys," she lied.

"I control this side of the border for them. If I can solve a problem the mob's having, the sky's the limit. You see? I have something on a guy in our local police force. He keeps me informed of what's going on."

"Wow, what's going on, sweetie?"

"Jesus, Cheri. You ask some dangerous questions. All I can say is there's a pile of gold at the end of the rainbow and there are a lot of us with picks and shovels. We've been doing a lot of digging. There was a guy who wouldn't cooperate and knew too much. He's no longer among the living. I'm trying to tell you, sweetie, don't get too nosy."

Did this guy happen to be Albert? He's not around anymore. It was like doing a jigsaw puzzle; first you form the border, than fill in the middle.

His head started to nod and his eyes lost focus. She was a little tipsy herself. She slowly picked up her purse and walked out, trying not to sprain her ankle as she maneuvered through the crowd in her four-inch spikes. She glanced back when she got to the door. Riley's head was on the bar. He was sleeping.

Good, she thought. The chances he'll remember what he said looked to be in her favor.

The next morning she parked the car and walked the one block to work. Thunder roared in the distance and flashes of lightening were getting closer. The rain started splattering on the sidewalk. The wind pulled at her umbrella and she struggled with her balance. She ran downstairs into the office. Her wet blouse and skirt clung to her and dripped water all over the floor. Sitting silently in the dimly lit basement, Bogart had a sheepish look and sported one hell of a shiner. What in hell had he gotten into now, she thought. I'm certainly not going to ask.

"Where in hell's Jimmy? He was supposed to be here thirty minutes ago," Bogart said with a voice that sounded like a handful of Gillette razor blades grinding.

"I think that's him," Clover said, as she heard the door open after a brief knock.

"Sorry, folks. The bus I started out with broke down," Jimmy said as he ran down stairs.

"What in hell happened to you?" Jimmy couldn't help grinning, as he looked Bogart up and down. "Did some husband catch up with you? I see why you didn't get to Albert's sendoff."

"It's a long story that I'm not going to get into, and it hurts like hell and Mother's on my case. She figures I'm into the sauce again."

"Are you?"

"Hell, no. It was an accident; besides, that's one hell of a personal question. I don't want to hear any more about it. Cut out the bullshit, I'm your lawyer; and another thing, you haven't made a payment for a month."

Who pissed in his cornflakes? "Sorry, Bogart, I'll pay you next week for sure."

"Things are getting serious. There's a lot of talk going around about a stash of gold. My sources say it might get bloody," Bogart said.

"Yeah, I heard something about that too. That big gold robbery might have been pulled by someone in town and hidden somewhere," Jimmy said, as he took a glance at Clover. He wondered if he should tell Bogart the story of the gold robbery. She gave a slight shake of her head that said keep your big mouth shut.

" I think it's a bunch of nonsense. That was big time. It sure as hell wasn't pulled by anyone from our sorry part of the world," Bogart said as he opened his desk drawer for an aspirin bottle and swallowed a couple of pills.

"Ray's murder investigation has gone cold," Bogart said. "We have to get the cops more involved. The police regard Ray as just another small-time crook. They're not going to spend much time trying to figure out who killed him. Do you know Ray's family?"

"I know of them. Why?" Jimmy said.

"I heard they're prominent people in Toronto. Mr. Baxter's a banker, former lawyer and fund-raiser for the Conservative

Party. My idea is for you to visit them, see if they would use their connections to put some pressure on the law."

"I'm not fussy about it, but it should be done," Jimmy said.

"Do you want to go with him, Clover? I figure he'd need a little help."

"As long as he behaves himself," Clover laughed.

Damn, this is my lucky day. Traveling to Toronto with the most beautiful girl in Windsor, thought Jimmy.

"Let's see if we can make an appointment with Ray's parents first," Clover said.

I hoped she had a plan; Jimmy had no idea how to proceed. He tried to remember Ginger's story of the family. They lived in a big house in a ritzy area. He was a businessman and she was a society lady.

"They lost a son, Jimmy. You have to tell the truth and not fill them full of your bullshit. Don't hurt them any more than they have been already," Bogart said.

Jimmy frowned. "I'll do my best. I'll be at home waiting to hear from you, Clover."

"Okay, figure on leaving tomorrow morning," Clover said. "I'll call you and confirm as soon as I can."

Having made the appointment, to see Ray's mother and father, for ten o'clock the following day, Jimmy and Clover set out for Toronto in her coupe. With the heavy traffic on two-lane Highway 2, it was slow and dangerous; cars and trucks passing with very little space and tailgating made Jimmy nervous. It would make a hell of a difference when the new highway was finished. Jimmy didn't mind the slow drive. Clover looked quite ladylike with a pink blouse buttoned up to her neck, a long skirt and wearing a wide-brimmed straw hat. Her earrings matched her blouse. She was a very good singer and seemed to know every country song as she serenaded him. She even sounded a bit like Patsy Cline.

"They live in the Bridle Path area," Clover said. "The directions Mr. Baxter gave me should make it easy to find. We'll stay at a hotel for the night and be ready for the morning meeting,"

"Sounds good to me, " Jimmy said. Dealing with rich people wasn't his cup of tea. He felt intimidated. You don't meet too many big shots in the sticks. The only ones he met were tourists going hunting or fishing with enough gear to outfit everyone in town.

The thought of spending the night with Clover made it all worthwhile. How lucky could one guy get? The one time that they spent the night together, the moon was shining on the lake, shadows danced on the wall and a loon called in the distance. He felt as if he had gone to heaven. He hoped he wouldn't be so nervous this time.

The night clerk at the motel had given them a suspicious look. Jimmy signed in as Mr. Delaney and wife. Maybe the clerk sensed they weren't married. Anyway, it was none of his damn business. This crummy hotel probably needed the money. Their room on the second floor had seen better days. The worn blue bedspread and gray towels matched the threadbare carpet. The smell of ammonia made it seem clean but the dust and cobwebs in the bathroom told a different story.

Jimmy sat on the bed, and looked up at Clover when she left the bathroom and walked towards him. She stopped; her lips parted and her eyes shone as she slowly raised the baby-doll pajamas over her head. Her long black hair fell over her shoulders and entwined her breasts. Her brown eyes seemed to darken. The cast shadows across her body revealed more than they hid.

Jimmy took her hand and gently pulled her down on the bed.

CHAPTER 15

They rose early the next morning, quickly dressed and checked out, anxious to go to the Baxter's. There was a bounce in Jimmy's step as he took Clover's hand. He was gaining confidence; things were starting to happen. They walked across the street to the Mercury restaurant on Bay Street, sat at the counter and both ordered ham, eggs and coffee.

"Guess we're both hungry," Clover said.

"I'll be glad when this is over." He put jam on a piece of toast and ate half of it. "Let's get started."

They walked back to the parking lot. Jimmy unlocked the car and opened the passenger side door for Clover and said, "Just think; it could be like this for the rest of our lives. Just you and me against the world."

Clover smiled, "That's us, baby."

Jimmy dug the Toronto road map out of the glove box and handed it to Clover. "Here, you find it, you're better at it than me."

"Well, I do have the address."

The big two-story stone house stood on a corner. The perfectly trimmed hedge surrounded a lawn the size of two tennis courts. The grass was green and lush. A gardener was tending rose bushes along the front of the house.

Jimmy knocked and a maid in a black and white uniform opened the door.

"Good morning, we have an appointment with the Baxters," Jimmy said.

She led past a long foyer and into a library. Jimmy walked up to the large snooker table and couldn't resist rolling a ball towards a pocket; no wonder Ray was so good at the game, he could play all day. An oak table sat in a corner of the room with six padded chairs around it. He watched Clover walk over to examine paintings on the wall. She stopped in front of one with a green bottle, cut glass crystal wine glass and a bunch of purple grapes.

"This is signed R. Baxter."

"He told me he painted, maybe he should have stuck with it, "Jimmy said.

"My son was a very good painter." Jimmy and Clover turned towards a voice from behind them. A tall, thin, well-tanned man with receding grey hair, wearing dress pants, a shirt and tie walked towards them.

"He was very good," Clover said.

"Yes, but then it's tough making a living at it. I think he'd have made a fine lawyer." He motioned to the table "Please sit down. I'm Gordon Baxter, welcome to our home. My wife will be in shortly."

Guess he could be described as smooth. Not the usual Saturday morning get-up Jimmy was used to.

"Thank you," Jimmy said.

"He looked at Clover. Her face was flushed, her eyes were downcast as she said hello, and sat down.

A lady, wearing a cream-colored skirt and white blouse entered the library carrying a silver tray with a coffee pot, cups, sugar bowl and creamer and set it on the table. The maid followed with a tray of croissants and muffins, set it down, poured coffee and left the room.

"I appreciate you coming. I've been anxious to meet you, I'm Ray's mother, Jeannine," She had none of her husband's shine. Her eyes were red and puffy with lines at the corners and around her mouth. A few strands of blond hair fell over her forehead. Her hand shook as she picked up her coffee cup.

"Good morning, Mrs. Baxter. You have a beautiful home," Clover said.

"Thank you." Mrs. Baxter then picked up the tray and passed it around.

Clover looked at Jimmy, and gave him an encouraging smile.

"I'm Jimmy Delaney. Meet Clover Spence, my representative from the lawyer's office." Jimmy paused to collect his thoughts and took a deep breath. "First we want to offer our condolences."

"Thank you, we appreciate it," Mr. Baxter said.

"Thank you," Mrs. Baxter said.

"I've been Ray's friend for the past four years. I thought of him as a younger brother."

"Tell me about my son," Mrs. Baxter said, her voice breaking and with tears in her eyes.

"Ray wasn't a bad guy, Mrs. Baxter. He wanted thrills and excitement. It was all fun and games with him. Your son was well loved by everyone." Jimmy finished his muffin, sipped tea and continued. "The police investigation into his murder has grown cold and the police are working on the case as hard as they should and—"

"How can we help you in that regard?" Mr. Baxter interjected. "We're a long way from Windsor."

"Please listen to the young man, Gordon," Mrs. Baxter said.

"We think you can talk to people," Jimmy said.

"That's all well and good, Mr. Delaney. Why are you so interested?" said Mr. Baxter, looking at Jimmy with his piercing eyes.

"My client, Jimmy, and your son were close friends," Clover said. "They worked, travelled, even spent time in jail together. I believe he just wants to make things right and bring the killer to justice."

"He wasn't cut out for your world, Gordon, Mrs. Baxter said, pointing at him. "Looking back, we should have let him become whatever he wanted in life, rather than trying to force him to be part of ours."

Yeah, Jimmy thought. Ray sure had moved on. This place was like Mars compared to the life most of them lived.

"Dammit, Jeannine, we've been over this a hundred times," Mr. Baxter interrupted. Jimmy saw now that the man's polish had been just a thin facade, now washed away entirely. His voice shook and tears welled in his eyes. "I wanted him to be like me and that was wrong. I should've let him go to art school like he wanted."

Jimmy continued, hoping it would help Ray's parents with their grief. "Ray and I had many heart-to-heart talks, especially in jail," Jimmy said, looking around this imposing home, wishing he was somewhere else. "He knew what you wanted for him. He didn't begrudge it. He told me he loved you both and was sorry he disappointed you." He guessed he should have crossed his fingers, but it was mostly true anyway.

Mrs. Baxter was crying openly. Mr. Baxter was wiping his eyes, trying to hold it together. Tears were running down Clover's cheeks.

"Did he have a girlfriend?" Mrs. Baxter asked.

"He was very popular with the girls," Jimmy said. "His girlfriends were all very proper ladies." Why in hell did he lie like that? Who knows, a few white lies might be a good thing.

"Will you stay and have lunch with us?" Mrs. Baxter asked.

"No thanks," Jimmy said. "We want to get back to Windsor this evening." He just wanted to get out of there. There was enough sadness in the house to make a statue cry.

Mrs. Baxter hugged Clover, then Jimmy. There was a hint of a sparkle in her eyes and a smile on her face. Mr. Baxter nodded at Clover and shook Jimmy's hand.

With Mr. Baxter's promise to get the investigation into his son's murder on the front burner, they backed out of the long driveway and headed to Windsor.

There was a good stretch of quiet before Clover finally said something.

"They thought they were doing the best for their son, maybe Ray was destined for this anyway."

"He sure in hell had choices."

"We all did." Clover turned sideways and looked out the window at the slow-moving traffic.

What made Ray leave a life of privilege? He had everything going for him; everything handed to him on a golden platter. A life of crime may have looked glamorous and exciting at the time, but it sure as hell wasn't. Jimmy had found that out.

"I'm getting hungry, Jimmy, let's stop at London and look for a drive-in restaurant, and I feel like a hamburger." She stretched, yawned, sat up and turned the rearview mirror towards her face, put on lipstick and ran a comb through her hair.

"Sure, I'm hungry too."

As they drove on, there seemed to be a change in Clover. He remembered her tears at the Baxter place. Jeez, what had that been about? Clover didn't even know Ray. I thought she was a pretty tough dame. Well, maybe just on the outside.

They pulled into the drive-in and parked. There was a small lineup inside and three carhops running to delivering the orders.

"Jimmy," she said in a voice about as flat as the fields of corn along the highway. "We're getting nowhere. All I can see ahead is trouble. The more I get into this, the more I think that maybe the gold might not have been all that important to me. There's something missing here. I want a future. I'm thinking of going home for a while, my parents are getting old and I want to spend time with them."

Jimmy felt like he'd just been kicked in the ass by a runaway elephant. "Jesus, Clover, I thought we were pretty close. I was hoping this whole mess would blow over, and then we could make plans for our life together."

"I dreamt the same thing, but it's not happening like that." She paused, as if to confirm what she said. She looked at Jimmy again, "You just don't understand, do you?"

"Here's what I understand. I had a small fortune in gold hidden away. All we had to do was sell it, lay low for a while, then live the good life. Well, the gold's around somewhere."

"I'm not that hungry anymore, let's go straight to Windsor." She opened the door, slammed it shut and walked to the driver's side. "Move over, I'll drive."

"Jimmy sat and moved the radio dial. All he got was static. He turned to Clover. "You better slow down, sweetie, you're going to get a ticket."

"Please be quiet."

The rest of the drive was in silence. Jimmy figured the best thing to do was to keep his big mouth shut.

She stopped the car in front of Jimmy's apartment. Jimmy leaned over, gave her a smack on the cheek, got out and watched the car until it was out of sight.

CHAPTER 16

The next morning, Jimmy got up, raised the blinds and looked out of the window; the sun was almost directly overhead. He made a peanut butter and jam sandwich and a cup of tea. He plugged in his iron, pressed his pants on the kitchen table, got dressed and wandered down the street towards the Ambassador Bridge and sat on a bench in the park nearby.

He always screwed up everything he tried to do in his life, and now he was losing Clover, the only girl he wanted to keep forever.

The sunshine glanced off skyscrapers across the Detroit skyline. The Penobscot Building looked like a giant castle cased in a yellow glow. A big freighter slowly moved up the river and sailboats danced on the waves. Four boys appeared to be having the time of their lives as they dove off a pier into the river.

The clouds rolled in and covered the sun. Everything darkened to match his mood. His thoughts were as dismal as the long wail of a locomotive whistle he could hear in the distance, bringing back memories of things lost in time.

As he was leaving the park a car pulled up beside him.

"Hey, Jimmy, get in, gotta talk to you." There was Sergeant O'Connor, big as life, still looking like a four-day old hotdog.

"Hey, what's up?" Jimmy lowered himself into the passenger seat. What in hell did the Sarge want? The dumb bastard was in charge of the investigation into Ray's murder but didn't seem bright enough to co-ordinate a two-car funeral.

"Another old friend of yours met his maker, Jimmy. You did a good job at his send-off. Didn't think you had it in you."

"Albert did a lot to help his fellow ex-cons. A lot of them are on the straight and narrow because of him, including me. He was a friend of mine for a long time. How in hell did you know what happened?"

"We keep an eye on what's going on in this town. Orders came down from on high to find Ray Baxter's killer. I'm asking for your help."

Jimmy couldn't believe it. The trip to Toronto wasn't in vain.

"I've known Albert for a long time. I first met him when I was a rookie cop. He was a crook then and still was when he died," O'Connor said.

"Well I won't be. I'm a reformed criminal."

"Yeah, and there's a lady in the moon. We had a suspect in custody but had to release him." O'Connor lit up a cigar that blew smoke in Jimmy's direction.

Jimmy coughed. "Jesus. Can't you afford any better cigars than that?"

"We have a motive and need someone to collaborate it. How well do you know this guy Riley?"

"I have no use for the son-of-a-bitch. But you know damn well if I rat on him, I'll have to leave town. He has a hell of a lot of connections; Jimmy looked warily at O'Connor and decided to chance it. "Fingers even reaching into your department."

O'Connor was quick to jump on that. "Most of us are honest. A few at the top may be crooked, but they're about to fall, if we get to the bottom of this. I might be a rough bastard but I'm as honest as a cop can be in this town. Windsor is an open city, Jimmy. The bad guys just do what they want. I don't like it, but that's the way it is. You work with what you have."

"What are you doing about Albert Arcand's killing?"

"I have no evidence yet but my gut tells me there's some kind of connection to Ray's murder. I think one thing will lead to another. Think things over, Jimmy. Hope you'll give this a second thought. You might be saving your own ass."

"Don't hold your breath."

Jimmy had learned several things over the last few years: you don't squeal on anyone; you mind your business, and take the bad with the good. But this situation was different. Things were getting murky. There wasn't much difference between the good guys and the bad guys. What did happen to Ray? Jimmy wished he could walk down to the Temple and talk this over with Albert, but those days were over.

"Call me if you change your mind," O'Connor said.

Jimmy left the police car and continued to his rooming house.

His room was hot as hell, even with the strong breeze blowing in through the open window and the fan running full blast. Jesus looked down on him, from the picture, with contempt. "You're a coward Jimmy. Your partner in crime, Ray, was murdered. Be a stand up guy. Do the right thing,"

I need a rest, thought Jimmy.

CHAPTER 17

After five rings, Ray's former girlfriend answered the phone.

"Hello."

"Hey, Ginger, this is Jimmy."

"Yeah, I know your voice. What can I do you for?"

"The cops picked up Riley yesterday for questioning. Did they call you?"

"Yeah."

"They had to let him go. Not enough evidence."

"I know."

"Jesus, Ginger, this is like pulling teeth. What did they want?"

"They want me to appear in court as a witness for the prosecution and to swear that Ray told me about the meeting he was going to have with Riley. I'm scared, Jimmy, although I would like to see Riley swing for this murder."

"So would I, for Ray and Albert Arcand. Guess you can say, they were my best friends."

"You know Ray talked about a guy named Albert. He said he would do something for him when he came into this windfall he talked about."

Yeah, that windfall was half mine, Jimmy thought. "I'd strongly suggest you don't testify, Ginger. Those mob guys play for keeps, and our great police-force sure as hell can't protect you."

"I'm thinking about it. I want to get even. I loved Ray and he said we were going to start on a great journey to reach our destiny." Her voice broke.

Reach our destiny. Jesus. Only Ray could get away with that bullshit. Jimmy had to admire him just the same. He sure had a way about him.

"Well, it's up to you, Ginger. Call me if there's anything I can do."

"I think you're trouble, Jimmy. But thanks anyway." She hung up the phone.

Jimmy glanced up again at the picture hanging on the wall. The disapproving look on Jesus' face was gone but he still didn't look happy. Still, Jimmy felt a little better. He had Clover on his mind. He had to talk to her. He dialed Bogart's office number and waited for what seemed forever.

"Smithers Law Office, Bogart speaking."

"Hello, Bogart. This is Jimmy. Can I speak to Clover?" Jimmy tried to keep his voice normal; he hoped Clover hadn't moved on.

"She's gone out for a bowl of soup. She gave me two weeks notice yesterday. What in hell went wrong? Did you screw up again? I knew she was sweet on you."

Jimmy's heart sank like a two-ton boulder into quicksand. He had hoped she was just tired, felt blue and would get over it.

"Life's tough and gets worse, Jimmy. Forget about Clover, your life is screwed up enough as it is."

"Dammit, Bogart. I don't need anyone telling me what to do," Jimmy barked and slammed the phone down. Every son-of-a-bitch and his brother were trying to run his life. Christ, they all sounded like his mother.

He propped up a pillow, lay down on the bed and picked up a *Liberty* magazine, leafed through it then threw it on the floor. The one beer left in the fridge didn't do him a damn bit of good. He needed a whole case.

His thoughts went back to his childhood: Head out with his friends into this exciting world. See how far they could swim along the shore. Catch minnows with their t-shirts to use for fish bait. Fish off the rocks across the lake then head home for a sandwich. Go into the bush with his slingshot and shoot at anything that moved. Never hit very much, but it sure was fun. Big dinner, then listen to The Lone Ranger on the radio. Everything was excitement and fun when you were eight. Well. I'm not a kid anymore. Where in hell do we go wrong along the way?

Jimmy eyes blinked and he jumped when the phone rang. "Hello?"

"Jimmy, I feel I owe you an explanation. Want to go for a drink?"

"Sure." What in hell did Clover think? The sunlight streaming in, reflecting on his wooden table and linoleum floor appeared brighter.

"I'll pick you up. Lets go to the Elmwood Casino. I'm leaving the office in about an hour."

"I'll be waiting out on the sidewalk," He saluted the picture of Jesus hanging on the wall. "I owe you one," he said. He shadowboxed across the room, feigned and dodged at an imaginary foe.

He took a bath, shaved, changed clothes, walked out and leaned back on a lamppost with his hands in his pockets: whistling and sometimes singing. An old guy passing by looked at him strangely.

He heard Clover's car before he saw it; it needed a new muffler. When the car stopped he jumped in, leaned over and kissed her on the cheek and said, "How are you, sweetheart?"

"Don't sweetheart me, Jimmy. Things aren't going to change."

They rode in silence to the Elmwood Casino. That's where the big stars performed: Sophie Tucker, Ted Lewis, Jimmy Durante and a slew of others. Most were big names from the dying days of vaudeville.

Jimmy ordered his usual, a roast beef sandwich and a beer. Clover just wanted a Manhattan. Her white pillbox hat with a tiny veil, black flowered dress, white high-heeled shoes and white gloves gave the appearance of a high-class dame out for a drink. The frayed sport coat he wore was the only one he had, his white shirt needed pressing and his tie had gravy on it. Although he had polished his shoes and shaved, he figured she'd be ashamed to be out with him.

An ashtray and small bowls of flowers, on white table-cloths, decorated the table in the Cantonese Room. Heavy brocade drapes kept the room dark and cool.

" I'm having a tough time with this. I'm no prize, but I thought we had something going." Jimmy said.

"We did. Maybe we still do. I'm tired of this life, always looking over my shoulder, looking for an angle." She waited until the waiter set the drinks down then continued. "I've saved a bit of money and want to go back to school. I have enough good marks from high school to get into Teachers College. After I finish visiting my family, that's where I'm heading." She had a determined look that Jimmy knew meant business.

"What about the gold?" Jimmy said.

"There's more to life than money. Who knows where in hell the gold's gone. Maybe it's already sold on the black market."

"If it was, I think we'd have some idea. Nobody we know has started to throw money around, or moved away. Those Detroit bastards are still around looking. The gold must still be under lock and key."

"Funny you should say that Jimmy. I still have the train tickets and the key you found in Ray's apartment. I stuck them in the safe."

"Jesus, Clover, I didn't mention the letter Albert left with his other belongings." He reached into his pocket, and pulled out a crumpled sheet of paper and handed it to her.

"Jimmy, you are a dumb ass!" She looked around the room, back at Jimmy, and then read in a low voice; *Look in bus or train station.* You must have some idea what this means?"

It started to dawn on Jimmy. They had a key with the number 359 engraved on it. "That's it!"

"Maybe I can help you, Jimmy."

"That's super," Jimmy said. He was back in her good graces and finally had a lead on the gold.

After another drink, Clover was in a good mood. She laughed and teased, her usual self. They left before the cover charge. Would've liked to see Johnny Ray, but couldn't afford it. Jimmy said goodnight when she stopped the car in front of his crummy rooming house. He thought about inviting her up to his room but figured there was no sense pushing his luck.

CHAPTER 18

Clover opened the door to her coupe and stepped out on the curb behind Bogart's office. An aura was emanating from the world around her. She was in a buoyant mood. She had given her two-week notice and couldn't wait for the last day.

She figured she owed Jimmy. She was the one who volunteered to help him sell the gold. Did everyone have the desire to get rich? Maybe she was a little too high and mighty. She wasn't the little girl from the sticks anymore.

The first hint of cool weather took the haze away. The sky was overcast, the humidity had risen and it looked like a morning rain.

A hand was gently placed on Clover's shoulder and a soft, high-pitched voice said, "Come with us and don't make a sound." She screamed and pulled away. An arm was wrapped around her and a hand covered her mouth. She was dragged to a car and pushed down into the back seat and the assailant followed her in. What is happening to me? For a brief instant, her thoughts reached out to her family, to Jimmy, then a paralyzing fear. What had she gotten into?

A dapper little guy sat down beside her. His hand was still holding her by her jacket. He had a thin moustache and smelled of Old Spice and old beer. A big bruiser with a pearl gray hat was in the driver's seat and the car slowly pulled away.

"Don't be afraid, sweetheart. We're not going to hurt you, although we can't guarantee no one else will," the little guy said, He smiled without showing any teeth and his eyes looked stone cold. He sent chills right through her. "My name's Marvin. My buddy behind the wheel is Henry."

"How did a hot dame like you get mixed up in this shit?" Henry said as he turned and looked at her.

Everything was a blur, Clover's voice constricted when she tried to scream and her body was shaking violently.

"What do you think, Marvin? Should we stop for a little action before we make the delivery?"

"It would be fun," Marvin chuckled. "But we were told to deliver her the same way we found her."

"What's this all about?" she screamed and kicked at Marvin.

"Just sit still, sister. No one can hear you," Marvin said.

"Stop right now and let me out."

Marvin and Henry laughed.

She quit struggling and looked out at her surroundings. Fields appeared and the houses receded behind her. She sat back. Her breathing returned to almost normal but the pit of her stomach felt like a lead balloon.

The car turned off onto a gravel road that ran between trees and stopped in a gravel parking lot, behind a low cement block building, just out of sight of the highway. The roof sagged in the center and the color of the stucco on the walls had turned a dark gray. The paint on the door and around the windows was faded and chipped. The grounds were made up of uncut grass and weeds, and partially surrounded by tall maple trees.

Marvin took her arm, pulled her out of the car, and led her into the building and down a long corridor to a small room. He opened the door and shoved her inside.

"Riley!"

Riley sat behind a battered desk; part of it piled high with automotive magazines and small motor parts. A few cardboard boxes, a stepladder and assorted junk littered the floor. The place smelled of oil, gas and grease.

"Cheri? Or… is it… Clover?"

Shaken and bewildered, all she could do was stand there tongue-tied.

"You sure had me fooled." Riley shouted, spitting the words out. "All along I thought we were friends. You could have had a good life with me, Clover. Instead you played me for a patsy."

He turned and looked at Marvin and Henry. "I have another job for you. Pick up our friend Delaney and bring him here. I don't know where he lives but chances are he's at the Temple.

"What in hell is this all about, Riley?" Clover said, her voice biting and harsh. She sat on the one remaining chair opposite Riley. Color returned to her face, her mouth had stopped quivering and she felt the determination to get through this.

"I'm an investigator for a lawyer working on a case that doesn't concern you at all. So what am I doing here?"

"I saw you with Jimmy Delaney at Albert's sendoff. You have information I want, and besides I don't appreciate being made a fool of."

"I didn't see you there."

"Do you think something that big would happen without me knowing?"

"Jimmy is just one of our clients," Clover said. "He hired us to help solve his friend's killing."

"Ray was a buddy of mine. He worked for me until he screwed up stealing mob money. You just don't do that and expect to live."

"I know you didn't shoot him."

"I didn't, but how do you know that?"

"It wasn't a mob hit. They don't use .25 caliber pistols and leave them at the scene. Even the cops don't believe you did it or they would charge you."

"Hey, maybe you're right. They picked me up then let me go. But that's not the reason I had you brought here, Clover. He picked up a broken piece of a piston rod and threw it across the floor. "You know too damn much. Do you think I don't remember our meetings?"

"I don't know anything about you Riley. We talked about your boyhood and your ambitions. That's all. You were more interested in getting in my pants."

The phone rang before he could reply.

"Riley, here." Small beads of sweat appeared on Riley's forehead. His hand holding the phone shook.

"I'm doing the best I can, boss. Okay, I'll be there in an hour." His face had a haunted look when he hung up the phone. "Now, what in hell am I going to do with you, Clover?"

"You can let me go. I'll find my own way home."

"Fat chance. I want you here when I return. You might figure some way to get out of here before I'm back. I'm going to be real upset if you do and have to track you down again. Don't get into any trouble while I'm gone." He smiled and chuckled to himself as he walked out of the building and locked the door behind him.

As the car sped away, she stayed sitting down. *How in hell am I going to get out of here*? She picked up the phone. Now what's Jimmy's number?" Damn if she could remember. She dialed O and waited for the operator to come on the line.

"Bell telephone, Agnes speaking."

"I'm looking for a phone number for James Delaney in Windsor."

"Just a moment, please…there are three of them."

"He lives on Wyandotte Street."

"Thank you… do you want me to dial the number for you?"

"Please, but give me the number for next time." Clover felt relieved. Hopefully, she would talk to Jimmy. He'd know what to do.

"Yeah," Jimmy answered.

"Oh, Jimmy, I've been kidnapped." Clover stifled a sob and her voice broke. She tried to control the panic that swept over her.

"What? What in hell happened?"

"I was picked up by a couple of mob guys and they brought me to Riley. I'm in an old building."

"Where?"

"It looks like an old garage out in the middle of nowhere."

"I'm coming to get you."

"I don't know where I am."

"Where's Riley? I'm going to kill him."

"Someone called and he left to meet him. It sounded to me like one of his bosses. He sent those two Detroit bastards who picked me up to find you and bring you here. He told them to look for you at the Temple. Stay the hell out of there. You have to go into hiding right now." Clover squared her shoulders and sat up straight. "They're after the gold! Don't worry; I think Riley will have second thoughts about me. We seem to be getting along."

"Call the police."

"They wouldn't know where I am either," she said.

"You have to get out of there before Riley comes back, I don't trust him any further than—"

"I'm in a real jam here. I'll try." She hung up the phone.

Clover looked around in desperation. She walked around the room, breathing heavily, lightheaded and her heart racing. She ran to a side door and pounded it with her fist, then picked up a heavy wrench, lying on the floor, and kept hitting the door handle until it broke. She opened the door. It led to a garage. There was a model A Ford, with no motor and flat tires, in a corner. Tires were piled beside it. For a fleet second she thought of her dad's old car that she had learned to drive. The garage door was locked and the two side windows had bars across them. She returned to the office and walked into the washroom, turned the handle on a door beside the wash-basin and it opened into a storage room. The only light was what came in through the door she had opened. She walked further into the room. There was a faint sliver of daylight from behind cardboard boxes piled almost to the ceiling. She ran back into the office and grabbed the stepladder, returned and set it up beside the boxes, climbed up three steps and began pulling them down. She cleared a path to a locked window. She ran back into the office, picked up a motor part on the floor, ran back and smashed the windowpane and cleared out the glass.

She pulled the stepladder close to the window and climbed out headfirst and tumbled onto the ground among the weeds and gravel. Damn, the outfit's all dirty and the silk stockings are ruined. She got up on her knees, turned her arm and looked at the blood on her scratched elbow and arm, and rubbed her shoulder until the pain gradually subsided. She picked up her shoes that had fallen off, and ran up the dirt road to the high-way. Which direction was Windsor? She glanced down and noticed the tire marks in the mud. They had turned left. She ran that way. The light rain, more like a drizzle, increased. Her shoulder began to throb and she felt chilled.

The drone of a vehicle increased, and the squeal of brakes sounded, as it approached a bend in the road. Clover stopped and looked around. There was nothing for a hundred yards except the blank faces of old buildings and empty parking lots. She thought of the two Detroit mobsters and Riley.

A truck veered around the corner and was going past her when the driver jammed on the brakes. A thick cushion of mud rose up from the road and a smell of burning rubber.

The truck door swung open. A kid stuck his head out. He was maybe eighteen, tops. "Hi lady," he said. "You want a ride to town?"

Clover recovered from the shock and studied the young driver. He had freckles, red hair and a wide friendly grin.

"Aren't you an angel," she said. "How far are you going?"

"Right into town. Got a load of corn for the market."

Clover climbed up into the cab, holding her high-heels. The kid seemed to be mesmerized by her long shapely legs.

"You sure came along at the right time. I've been walking for ages. My car broke down over in a side street about two miles back. What's your name?"

"Everybody calls me Billy. My real name is Guillaime, that's French for William." He kept glancing at the outline of her breasts through the wet blouse.

"Keep your eyes on the road, Billy, let's deliver the corn."

He turned red and they both laughed.

"You look like you had a fight with a grizzly bear," he said.

She didn't say anything. She slouched in the seat. Her shoulder was sore and the cuts and bruises on her face and legs hurt like hell. She started to shiver and tried to catch her breath.

Billy's face had a quizzical look. He shoved his cap back on his head and shut off the radio. "Can I do anything?"

"Yes, please drive me home."

"Sure thing."

"I'll tell you where to go."

Billy drove the truck to her apartment, stepped out, ran around and opened the passenger door. Clover picked up her shoes, stepped down and gave him a peck on the cheek and walked to her apartment.

She quickly stripped off the wet clothes, pulled down the bed covers and lay down. She felt bewildered and unhinged. There were thoughts of Riley and his two henchmen, the dream catcher and her grandfather. Images of Jimmy faded in and out of her dreams.

The room was dark when Clover awoke, very thirsty and with a headache. Her body was sore all over. Where was she? A gradual sense of what happened filtered through her mind. She rose from the bed and looked at the mud and blood on the sheets and over her body. She limped to the kitchen, swallowed two aspirin and water. She ran the bath water and slowly sank down into the tub. The steam rose from the water and the mirror clouded over. Her muscles relaxed and the pain subsided.

Clover dried herself, put on her robe, gathered the bed sheets and went out of the apartment and down the hall to the laundry room. Thoughts of Jimmy entered her mind. Who knows what he'd be up to. She went back to the phone and called him. After five rings someone picked up the phone. There was silence.

"Is this you, Jimmy?"

"Thank god, it's you. I'm sick with worry over you. Where are you?"

"I'm in my apartment. I got away. Those no-good bastards don't know where I live, at least I hope not. I thought I told you to get the hell out of town?"

"I couldn't while you were God knows where. Jesus, Clover, I was one worried bastard."

"Well, I'm safe at the moment. I'm shook up but going to be okay. We have to make plans, Jimmy."

"I want to see you."

"We haven't got time. I'll look for the gold. It won't take long to check out the bus and train stations. You take the train to Wishart Falls and hide out. I'll meet you there. Now don't give me a hard time, just do what the hell I tell you. I love you, Jimmy."

"I want to come with you."

"God dammit, Jimmy. Just do what I tell you."

"I'm leaving right now."

CHAPTER 19

A smile crossed Jimmy's face and his chest swelled and he pumped his fist in the air. Clover was safe. He heated up a can of tomato soup and made tea, he hadn't eaten since yesterday.

He called the railway station. A train to Toronto was due to leave at seven in the morning.

He looked out of the window at the dark outline of the Detroit skyscrapers against the faint light of the grey sky. He hated leaving. A city of hard-working, hard-living men and women, it was no place for sissies. He thought of himself and Ray driving from Windsor through the tunnel to the 509 nightclub on Friday night to watch the big name entertainers, or to a ballgame at Briggs Stadium to watch pitcher, Hal Newhouser and third baseman, George Kell. That part of his life was over and another phase was beginning.

Jimmy set his alarm clock for five thirty and went to bed. He woke up before the alarm clock sounded, packed his suitcase, and checked his wallet. His rent was paid up. There was just enough dough for a cab ride to the station and a ticket to Wishart Falls.

He opened the rooming house door, stopped, turned back and reached up for the faded picture of Jesus, opened his suitcase and laid it gently on top of his clothing. *You're coming with me, Jesus; I may need you.* Jesus seemed to smile. He closed the door and walked downstairs.

He paced the sidewalk with the suitcase in one hand and a half-eaten cheese sandwich in the other. Where in hell is the taxi? It finally rolled up. He took one last look at his two-floor rooming house; grey imitation brick siding, dirty windows and the weed-covered yard. He sure wasn't going to miss this place

Jimmy breathed a sigh of relief when the train pulled away from the station to start the ten-hour trip home. He looked out the window at the city of Detroit across the river; it was fast-paced and full of action. He was going to miss it. He thoughts turned to good memories and bad. Friends were gone and new enemies had appeared. Ray the party guy, was dead: always with a joke and surrounded by women. Memories of time spent in jail together; and the biggest high of all, stealing two bars of gold.

He got off the train at Union Station in Toronto. He walked across the street to Child's, for pie and coffee, then returned and boarded the transcontinental train. He sat next to the window in the coach, anxiously waiting for the train to leave.

He knew it was too dangerous to stay with Clover. Riley would have his men looking for a man. Did Riley know about the key?

The train started to move and picked up speed as it headed north and the factories and houses disappeared from the window, to be replaced by farmers' fields. The white smoke poured out of the stack of the engine and the sound of the whistle brought back memories of his childhood. He used to stand on the side of the tracks watching the trains pass, wave at the engineer and watch men dressed in suits and ladies in dresses sitting in the dining car. Where were they going? Someday he was going to travel to those faraway places.

No one sat beside him. After the conductor took his ticket, he walked to the smoker and enjoyed a cigarette. A traveling salesman kept the passengers in a jovial mood, with his jokes and tall tales. Jimmy wished he had that ability.

He returned to his coach, ordered a ham and cheese sandwich and a coffee. When he finished eating, he stretched his upper body across the seat and dozed off.

"Wishart Falls, Wishart Falls next stop." The conductors voice woke him up. He sat up with a cramp in his leg and his left arm numb. He grabbed his suitcase and limped off the train.

The wooden sidewalks and the high storefronts hadn't changed. There were long shadows from the buildings over the sandy streets. The wind kicked up gum wrappers, pieces of paper and dry leaves that swirled around. Any feelings he had for this place were long gone. There were too many memories of failure. Those days are over. He thought of Clover on her journey.

He turned off the road from the station and looked over at his mother's store. It looked smaller than he remembered.

The faded sign over the door, Delaney and Son was readable in the failing daylight. The gas lamp lit up the store and he could see the outline of his mother sitting by the cash register. She would be tired.

He opened the screen door to the store, poked his head in, and shouted, "Hey Ma."

"Jimmy!" she shouted, rushed over and cried as they embraced. "I'm so glad you came home. I was expecting you to write."

"I'm sorry, Ma. I'm going to be here for a while. Thought I'd stay at the cottage. Maybe I can help out in the store and do a few chores around the place."

"That would be wonderful, son. I'm getting old. These days you can't find good help. It's not like it used to be in my day. Where's Clover?"

"I expect her here in a day or so."

"She's a wonderful girl. Don't let her go."

"I expect to marry her, Ma."

"That would be wonderful. We could have the wedding in our church. Is she Protestant?"

"Hmm … I think so."

"Then a big reception at the Lion's Club. We'll invite the whole town. Oh, I can't wait."

"Yeah, okay, Ma." He thought there was no use getting into it. Once women hear even a faint tinkle of wedding bells there's no stopping them. Besides, it might not even happen.

"I'm going to close up now and visit your father's grave. We'll bring flowers."

"That'll be fine. I think of him a lot."

"So do I. He was a fine man until he came home from the war. I remember our wedding day as if it was yesterday. The reception was held at the home of our dear friends. I don't think his mother ever liked me. We cleared the furniture out of the parlor and danced until dawn. We hitched up the team the next day and drove downtown to look at the lot where we were going to build our home."

"That was a long time ago, Ma. Let's look to the future."

"I'm getting up in years, Jimmy. I just pray to God, you'll come to your senses and make a life for yourself here."

Jesus, this was going to be tough.

"You and Clover can run the store. I would be free to help with the children."

"Ma, I don't want to live here. I've told you a hundred times." There was no use getting upset. It wasn't going to change and maybe you couldn't blame her. Her one and only son, in and out of jail, who ran a poker joint and appeared to have no future. Well he does now, a small fortune in gold, and a beautiful girl.

They walked down a well-worn path to the graveyard. His mother picked a small bouquet: daisies, buttercups and black-eyed susans from the fields. They passed the Catholic graveyard and the wire fence between it and the Protestant site. On the side of a slight hill covered with blueberry bushes a small wooden cross that marked a raised grave. Jimmy and his mother picked out the weeds and grass and lay the flowers on it. He put his arms around his sobbing mother and tried not to cry.

Jimmy glanced at his mother as they walked home in the twilight. The frown was gone, and her eyes sparkled as she hummed a song.

"I'm very happy you're home, son.

"So am I."

His mother's macaroni loaf and apple pie brought back memories of a simple time. Jimmy didn't have a worry in the world back then, he just wanted to get out of town.

Jimmy filled a box with groceries from the store and left for the cottage. The ten-minute drive reminded him of the night he and Clover stayed there. They had made love for the first time. It was magic.

He parked, picked up his suitcase and walked to the cottage door, fumbled with the key in the darkness, entered the house and lit the kerosene lamp. The light flickered and the shadows leapt on the pine walls. Outside the sky had swallowed the sun. The only sounds were the hooting of an owl and the sound of a loon. He found a flashlight and went back to the car for the groceries.

The bedroom was stuffy and warm. Jimmy opened the window, undressed and went to bed. It was hard and lumpy but felt welcome anyway. He tossed and turned for an hour, then fell into a troubled sleep. It had been a long day.

"Wake up Jimmy." A female voice echoed and a light tried to penetrate the dreamlike state he was in. He turned on his side and pulled his legs up closer to his body and burrowed further under the blanket. The bed shook and the voice was heard again, "Jimmy, wake up." He turned to the light and tried to focus his eyes. What the hell was that? The first thing he saw was a reflection from the lamplight glittering on what appeared to be a small gold cross on a gold chain.

"What the hell," he shouted and sat up.

"Hello, Jimmy."

"Audrey!"

She held the lamp in one hand and a hunting rifle in the other. Tears streaked down her cheeks. Her hair was uncombed and her eyes appeared vacant and dead. Her mouth had a faint smile. She set the lamp down on the dresser, raised the rifle, and pointed it at Jimmy.

"Audrey! What in hell's going on?"

"Stay right there, Jimmy."

"Jesus, Audrey, put the gun down. What's the matter with you?"

"I want the gold."

"What gold?"

"The gold you and Ray stole and hid here."

"I haven't got it. Someone beat me to it."

"That was Ray and I. He didn't know where the cottage was but he knew you had the gold buried behind the outhouse." The rifle lowered in her hands. She quickly brought it up again. "He asked me to bring him here. He dug it up. When we got back to Windsor he took up with Ginger and I was left out in the cold. Turns out he was just using me to get to the gold; the lying, cheating bastard." Her high-pitched laugh echoed throughout the room. Her eyes glistened in the lamplight.

"How did you know I was here?"

"News travels fast. Your mother told everyone who came into the store. You made her very happy."

"How in hell am I supposed to know where it is now?"

"Everybody in Windsor seems to think you have the gold."

"How was I supposed to find it?"

"Remember when you went to search his apartment?"

"There was no gold there. Did you ever think he might have hid it again?"

"I'm so confused."

"Put down the gun, Audrey."

I shot Ray and now I'm going to shoot you unless you tell me where it is."

Jimmy gasped and stared. "You didn't!"

"I did."

"You shot Ray...I can't fucking believe it...Why?"

"I went to see him. I wanted an explanation. He laughed at me. I picked up the revolver lying on the night table, pointed at him and it went off." Her voice trembled. "I didn't mean to do it, even though the lying son-of-a-bitch deserved it."

"Audrey, tell me you're lying."

He double-crossed me, and then threw me over. Men have screwed me over all my life, starting with my father beating me and calling me names. There were bad boyfriends, including you." She lowered the rifle again and brought it back up. "I thought Ray was different. Ray, the man I adored, left me for a little redheaded slut. I can't take it any more. I want money and hope to start a new life. No more men, no more broken promises."

"Put the gun down, Audrey."

"It's no fun, Jimmy. Waiting on tables in a crummy restaurant with some guy trying to slip you a feel, hoping to get in your pants, lousy tips and no one to come home to. Working in that crummy dime-a-dance place in Detroit. Men, drunk and smelly, give you a ten-cent ticket for a dance, then think they own you."

"You won't have any future if you shoot me, Audrey, you know that. The cops will put two and two together."

"I really don't give a shit. Jimmy. Now tell me where the gold is."

How in hell did I deserve this? Hiding from the mob that's chasing me, trying to find the gold, now Audrey. What kind of predicament did I put Clover in? Who knows where she is. It was one sad fucking day when Ray and I pulled the heist.

"Let's talk this over, remember you're the one who left me for Ray. You know I had a crush on you ever since grade school."

Drops of sweat appeared on her upper lip, Her body swayed, her arm dropped down and the rifle fell to the floor. She sat down on a chair and cried softly.

Jimmy walked over and put his arms around her.

The crying increased.

"It doesn't have to end like this, we can fix it," Jimmy said.

"Oh Jimmy, what went wrong? Remember when we started out for the big city? We were full of promise. We should have got married and stayed here; with you working in the store, and raising a family in a little house by the lake."

"We didn't want that then, Audrey, and we don't now. We have to make the best of it. That's all water under the bridge." Jimmy stopped shaking long enough to reach in his open suitcase for a bottle of Four Aces wine and poured two tumblers full. Memories flooded back. Two kids who didn't fit in and wanted more.

"I'm beat, Jimmy," she said with slurred speech. He led her to his bed; gently helped her lay down and covered her with a blanket. He picked up the rifle, walked over and put it back in the closet. He went outside with the wine bottle, sat on the porch steps and lit a cigarette.

A small streak of light appeared on the horizon and a mist rose from the lake. The only sound came from a slight rustling of blowing leaves and the beating of his heart.

What had he started? What force did he unleash on his friends and family? It wasn't supposed to end up this way.

He finished the bottle of wine, threw it in the bush and went back in the cottage, stretched out on the couch and fell asleep.

CHAPTER 20

After a night of tossing and turning, Clover slept in. Damn, she needed an alarm clock. She had hoped to get an early start in her search for the gold. She ate a bowl of cereal, drank a cup of coffee and started packing. This was not something she relished. Did she really have this many clothes? Her photographs, jewelry box, keepsakes and treasures she accumulated over the year's filled one suitcase. Dresses, slacks, blouses and underwear were jammed into another. Her shoes and hats filled a shopping bag.

She had two goals, find the gold and meet Jimmy. Thoughts of running into Marvin and Henry again made her shudder. Of course, this plan had a flaw. Of all the guys in the world, why did she fall for Jimmy? He wasn't marriage material. He didn't have a job and he was a thief. He was trying to become a better man and maybe his love for her would change him. Would her parents approve of him? No, they certainly wouldn't.

Clover picked up a key, with the number 359 stamped on it, from the table. According to Albert's note to Jimmy, it opened something at a bus or train station.

Because Riley and his two gunsels, Marvin and Henry, had seen her car, she figured it would be safer to travel around Windsor by bus. She found a housedress about two sizes too large for her in Dolly's closet. A kerchief over her head, flat bottom shoes, no lipstick and sunglasses weren't the greatest disguise, but it was the best she could do. She nodded in approval as she looked in the mirror. She wondered if her mother would recognize her.

Traveling by bus around Windsor was a new experience for her. She had both bus stations checked in an hour. The three railroad stations were spread across the city. She stopped at Woolworth's for a hamburger and coffee then continued. It was well into the afternoon when she entered the last one. There was no locker numbered 359 anywhere. An elderly ticket clerk looked her way and smiled as she approached the wicket. "Excuse me, mister. Would this key open a locker somewhere?"

"Hmm, where did you get it?" he said as he took it from her hand and turned it over.

"Ah… my brother mailed it to me and told me to pick up his clothes," she blurted out.

"Well, he must have mailed them to the wrong sister." He held the key up to the light of the window and studied it far too long. "A number this high tells me it's for a locker in a big station. Probably Toronto or Detroit. How do I know you didn't find this key?"

"My brother's moving to Toronto, I should have known; give me the key, please."

He handed it to her. Without saying a word Clover put it in her purse. The sound of her heavy shoes hitting the hardwood floor echoed throughout the station. She continued to a bus stop and boarded the Erie Street bus, returned to her apartment and changed clothes. She'd have to drive her car for the next leg of the journey, there was no choice.

She scribbled a quick note to her roommate.

Dear Dolly. When you read this, I'll be well on my way. Due to circumstances I can't mention, I have to leave town. I'm not coming back. The hundred dollars on the table will cover my share of the rent for the next three months. I hope you'll find a new roommate by then. I think of you as a dear friend and hope to see you again some day. The right man will come along. Please use everything I left behind. You'll look great in that green skirt.
   Clover.

Because of the heavy traffic on Highway 2, the drive to Toronto was as slow as a three-legged snail running up hill. She stopped at the same restaurant in Brantford where she and Jimmy had eaten on the way to visit the Baxters. It still looked pretty drab; dirty windows, worn-out linoleum but the food was good. A waitress rose from the staff table and slowly sauntered over with a glum look on her face. She popped her gum and with a dismissive look asked, "What you having?"

"A ham sandwich and coffee please," Clover tried to sound as snotty as the waitress. That's what Jimmy would have ordered.

The jukebox was blaring.

Till I waltz again with you
Keep my love locked in your heart
Darling, I'll return and then
We will never have to part.

Clover toyed with her coffee cup as she stared out the window. That song brought back memories: Jimmy snapping his fingers to the music on the jukebox and singing along with Theresa Brewer, reaching under the table and caressing her knee, then kidding around with the gum-popping waitress. Thinking of his long black hair and good looks made her feel like singing. Was that when she first fell for Jimmy? Yeah, like a million cupid arrows, but why? There had been a few men in her life but he was the only one that got her heart racing since Eddie.

She paid her bill and left the restaurant as the sun set behind the trees that lined the road. She stopped at a service station, where the gas jockey filled the tank, checked the oil and cleaned the windshield. She pulled back onto the highway as a cool breeze picked up and dark clouds threatened rain. It reminded her of early autumn on the prairies and the only worry she had was what elegant prince was going to sweep her off her feet and if they'd live happy forever. Was she going to live that way with Jimmy?

After an hour's drive she saw a faint light, in a clearing, from a sign that read Sleepy Hollow Inn. She turned off and drove two blocks to the motel: a cement block building with six rooms and a small office. The clerk looked her up and down with her unwelcoming cold eyes. "I want a room for the night," Clover said.

"That'll be three dollars."

Clover paid.

"Room number two."

Clover drove as close to the door of the room as she could. Her eyes lit up when she entered. It was freshly painted and the furniture was new. She quickly lugged the canvas bag into the room and locked the door. Relaxed and sleepy, she turned on the radio, found a station with dance music, undressed and got into bed with a romance novel. The writing on the page became a blur. She reached up, turned off the radio and fell asleep.

She woke early. Was the voice she heard during the night a dream? "Stay true to the teachings of our people." The last words her grandfather said when she left home. Her face had a puzzled look when she glanced at her face in the mirror. Who is this person? Was love worth this? Would Jimmy settle down or is in this only for the gold.

She bathed, changed into slacks and a silk blouse. She had to be fashionable; after all she was going to the big city.

Clover loaded up the car. The gold seemed to be getting heavier each time. She drove north, through small towns, fields and apple orchards to Toronto. She drove down Yonge Street, over to Bay and parked a block from the Toronto bus station. She walked through the crowd into the station, then to the lunch counter for a breakfast of oatmeal, toast, jam and coffee.

Clover took a deep sigh, her lips tightened and her eyes widened as she got up and walked to the lockers on a far wall. There was box 359! She reached in her purse for the key. She glanced around. No one was paying any attention to her. Her legs felt heavy and her heart was racing. The key didn't fit. She tried and tried again.

"Need any help, Miss?"

She turned. A young guy dressed in a cheap suit, white shirt with cufflinks and a bowtie smiled at her. He had a small moustache that didn't seem to grow that well, a brush cut and piercing blue eyes.

"No thanks." Her voice shook, "I'm okay."

"I notice you want to get into that locker awful bad. Must be valuable shit in there. Maybe I can help you?"

She didn't acknowledge him, just turned and headed out the door. She didn't have to explain herself to that idiot. As she got into her car, she looked back. The apprehension left and her breathing returned to normal. He hadn't followed her. Was this one of Riley's cohorts she hadn't seen before or some guy on the make?

The next stop was Union Station, a grand marble building with giant pillars at the entrance, a gateway to Canada. Who were all these people and where were they going? Why people rushed around like this was anyone's guess. It sure as hell wasn't like this back home. She got lucky again and found a parking spot on Front Street.

She walked in and down the wide stairs into the concourse and continued on to a long wall of storage lockers. There was no box 359. She slowly checked each locker but no dice. Where else could it be? A redcap pushing a baggage truck was passing by. "Are there any more lockers in the station," she asked.

"Yep, there's some in the departure area. He pointed at a stairs going down to the next level. "Just go down and turn left."

"Oh, thanks a million."

She walked down to the lockers and followed the numbers. There was locker 359. Her heart raced, her face had a hunted look and her hands shook. She glanced around at the people hurrying by, put the key into the lock, money in the slot and turned the key. The door opened! There was a canvas satchel with a brown leather top and a short leather handle sitting deep in the box. She closed the door, Beads of sweat appeared on her forehead and her breath became shallow. Clover looked around, no one paid any attention to her. She opened the locker door again. She removed a canvas bag from her purse, opened it and pulled the satchel into it and moved it out of the locker. It fell from her grasp and landed on the floor with a thud. The damn thing was heavier than a sumo wrestler. She picked it up with both hands, held it to her side and moved slowly to the car. She shoved it under the seat, then jumped in the car and locked the doors, took a few deep breaths and waited for her heart to quite racing. A dream catcher that hung from the rear view mirror caught her eye. Her grandfather had given it to her when she left home. Clover smiled. It was the protection she needed. She drove away and started the long drive north.

Clover started to feel more secure and her curiosity grew. She pulled into a parking lot just past Barrie, and drove the car to a far corner, as far away from any buildings as she could get. Not a soul in sight. This has to be the gold; it's too damn heavy to be anything else. She reached down and pulled out the canvas bag, opened it and looked at the satchel; it had a cheap lock on it. She got out of the car, ran over and picked up a small rock from under a tree and returned to the car. A few bangs and the lock sprung open. With a feeling of anticipation, dread and fear, she opened the zipper and there were the two bars of gold shimmering in the sunlight. After a few deep breaths, her hands stopped shaking. She closed the satchel and shoved the canvas bag under the passenger seat.

Being stopped by the cops for speeding or getting a flat tire would have been dangerous. Any unwanted attention to her or the car could bring disaster. Thoughts of Jimmy had a calming effect. He wouldn't want her to be frightened. She drove from the parking lot at a slow speed and turned north on highway 11. All she had to do was stop for gas and drive to Wishart Falls, and Jimmy. She turned on the radio and sang along with Kitty Wells. It made her feel better.

It was dark when she arrived in North Bay and checked into the Empire Hotel. It was expensive, but she felt the gold would be safer than in a crummy motel off the highway. Clover weaved her way, through a milling crowd, to the check-in counter. A banner hung from the ceiling read, Northern Ontario 1952 Mining Convention. Guys in suits and others in plaid shirts, breeches and high-top boots stood and sat in the lobby, sang, hollered and acted like jackasses. The few women attending were quite sedate but took everything in stride and enjoyed themselves.

"This is sure heavy. You don't travel light, lady," the bell-boy muttered, as he carried the canvas bag into the room.

"You don't know the half of it, buddy," she said and handed him a fifty cent tip.

As she sank down in the water in the bathtub, a chill ran through her body. Was it the too cool water or a reaction to an exciting day? The soft feeling of the cotton pajamas soon brought on a feeling of contentment. She had the gold and Jimmy was waiting. She shoved the bolt into the door lock and jammed the wooden desk chair under the doorknob. With the trip through Toronto behind her, she relaxed and sleep came quickly, only to be awakened by a ruckus outside the door. She burrowed deep down into the blankets, heart racing while re-citing the few prayers she learned in Sunday School.

After a few thuds and shouts, things returned to normal.

Morning came too soon. It was going to be another long day. If only she could phone Jimmy. The sound of his voice and reassurance was what she needed.

CHAPTER 21

It was a long drive to Wishart Falls from North Bay; north on Highway 11 for two hours, then another four hours after turning off onto a gravel road, with more twists and turns than a spooky radio show. The deep dark forest, fast-flowing rivers and deep blue lakes appeared to be in all the right places. Was this the work of Sky Woman who had fallen from a hole in the sky and brought order to Mother Earth? In the autumn, the prairies were painted yellow and brown, and ran forever, until it met a light blue sky. In the winter everything was white and gray, including the sky. Was that where she belonged? Maybe someday she'd return, but then where did Jimmy fit in? Would he be happy to settle down and live the life of a farmer? She knew he wouldn't.

Clover wished she had listened closer to the teachings of her grandmother. In the city she thought less about her roots. Out here, among the forest, lakes and fresh air, the stories that filled her childhood came flooding back. Her most vivid recollection was from a visit to her grandparents' cabin about five miles from the village. It was January and there was deep winter snow. The dog team seemed to take forever to get there.

She made a short run with her grandfather to his trap-line the next day, returning with two beavers.

"You're twelve years old now, Clover, its time for you to learn our ways," her grandmother said. "Now, you watch me skin this beaver, then you do the second one. Just make sure you don't cut through the pelt." With coaching, Clover finished it and didn't make any cuts, but it sure hadn't look like grandmother's. Her grandmother went on; "The first time I went out with my father on the trap-line and we were returning, I was told to load everything on the sleigh. I forgot the axe. He was very upset. The next morning when my father was leaving the cabin, he turned and hollered, "The axe is leaning on the side of the house right beside the door."

"My mother just grinned and said it must have been the Memigueisi."

"What's a Memigueisi? Clover asked.

"They're the little people that live by the river banks. They do good deeds, but at times they are real mischief-makers, and like playing tricks." My mother went over to the tobacco-can and came back with a small handful of tobacco. "Place it on a ledge by the big rock as a gift. It's best to keep on their good side. They can be a little nasty at times."

"Why do we do that? Clover asked.

"To give thanks. We always sprinkle tobacco over the animals we shoot. They sacrifice themselves so we can eat their meat and use their skin for clothing."

Clover remembered when she was about six years old and her grandmother made her a doll out of straw. When she got a bit older, her grandmother also taught her how to sew and cook. Would she have grandchildren some day?

Her mind was pulled back to Ontario and her present surroundings when she drove into a small village. She pulled off the road. There was a post office, a church, four or five weather-beaten log houses and an abandoned head-frame. She locked the car and walked up to a small log building. A sign on a pole in big letters above the door swung and creaked in the wind. Clover could make out the word Café, written in big letters.

She opened the door and entered a room that time had forgotten. A wood cook stove sat behind a long counter than ran the length of a wall. Three wooden tables, with two benches and assorted chairs, took up the space in the dining area. A picture of King George hung on one wall and a framed photograph of soldiers standing at attention was on another.

An old gentleman walked out of a small room beside the stove. He limped along with a cane, He had one good arm and his shirtsleeve was pinned up near the shoulder where the other arm used to be.

"Well, aren't you a pretty picture?" We don't get many young ladies stopping by, in fact, we don't get many of anybody," he said with a toothless grin.

"Hello, I'm famished." She sat at a table and asked, "Do you have a menu?"

"Nope. No need for one. I have beef and barley soup warming on the stove and I can make you a ham sandwich. There's rice pudding and apple pie."

"My favorites. I'll have the soup, pie and a cup of tea."

"Coming right up."

A short time later he set down her soup with his one arm, then returned with the pie and tea. "My name's Scotty and I hail from the highlands of Scotland," he said.

"I'm Clover and I hail from the western prairies."

They laughed.

The soup was excellent and the pie was as good as her grandmother used to make, and Clover told him so. She left a twenty-five cent tip and walked toward the door.

He followed her out. "Well, thank you. Have a safe journey and take care of yourself, lassie." He hesitated then said, "There was a young city slicker that stopped here about three hours ago. He asked me if by chance a pretty young woman driving a Ford coupe stopped by."

"I have no idea what that's about," she said and quickly unlocked and entered the car.

'Anyway, I told him all there was around here was wilderness. He said that was the last place he wanted to be and was going to head back south. His car had Michigan plates."

"Thanks, Scotty." Clover took a few deep breaths and waited until her heart stopped racing, rolled down a window and slowly drove away.

She drove behind a slow-moving truck loaded with logs. She didn't mind going slow, it's what was ahead that bothered her. The road ended in Wishart Falls.

The first thing that welcomed Clover into the village was a couple of large barking dogs that chased the car, but soon gave up. The only sign of life was a few children playing hopscotch in the school ground and a woman walking with a shopping bag.

She pulled up in front of the store, leaned over, looked in the rearview mirror and put on lipstick, rolled up the windows, got out and locked the car.

CHAPTER 22

Jimmy looked up from the cartons of cigarettes he'd placed on the shelf, when he heard the door open. There stood a vision he would never forget: Clover, with laughing eyes and a big smile. She spread her arms and he slowly walked over and embraced her, lifted her off her feet and swung her around. Her lipstick tasted of tangerine and she smelled of earth and sweat.

"We did it, Jimmy," she whispered, as she clung to him and tears welled up in her eyes.

"I know." Could this really be happening? Were his dreams finally come true?

"Ma, we have company," he hollered in the direction of the kitchen.

"Why, it's Clover. Oh, I'm so glad to see you," Mrs. Delaney said as she wiped her hands on her apron then hugged her.

"Anne, good to see you too. Thanks again for your hospitality on my last visit."

"I hope you're staying for a while. Jimmy might quit moping about. That boy can be the biggest pain at times."

"I'll take Clover to the cottage and get her settled in, Ma."

"That's fine, but let's eat first."

"Thanks. I am hungry." Clover said.

Jimmy smiled at he watched Clover set the table under the appreciative and caring eyes of his mother.

They enjoyed the cold meat sandwiches, butter tarts and lemonade.

Jimmy went back into the store and finished stocking shelves. The gold was in his possession and Clover was here. It's going to be busy for a while but nothing should stop them now. Drive to Santa Fe, sell the gold and hightail it to Mexico.

Jimmy hurriedly finished the job. He seemed to be floating. He could hear laughter coming from the kitchen.

"We're finished, Jimmy," Clover said.

"We better head out. Thanks for everything, Ma. We'll see you tomorrow."

Clover snuggled up to Jimmy as he drove the two miles to the cottage and filled him in on recovering the gold and her stay at the Empire Hotel. She didn't mention the city slicker.

Jimmy laughed and shouted like the cat from Alice in Wonderland.

He carried Clover's canvas bag into the cottage, opened it, took out the satchel, took one of the gold bars in his hand and raised it up. "My dreams are coming true. It won't be long, baby."

"We have a few things to do yet, Jimmy. We have to find a buyer and sell the damn stuff."

"All in good time, sweetheart."

They embraced and clung to each other. Jimmy picked her up in his arms and carried her to the bedroom. The moon wasn't shining through the window dancing on the walls like the first time, but their lovemaking was as joyous and wonderful. He could be lost in her arms forever.

Jimmy dozed off for what seemed like ten minutes. A slight wind blew through the open window. He looked over at the sleeping Clover. The shadow of the tree leaves was fluttering on her face. He hadn't been dreaming. He covered her with the sheet.

Clover had done it. She found the gold and brought it to him. He knew he couldn't retrieve the gold himself and that he had put her life in danger. She was safe now and he vowed to keep her that way. He closed his eyes and went back to sleep.

Birdsong and chirping chickadees, from the open window, woke up Jimmy. He glanced at his wristwatch: nine o'clock. He leaned over and kissed Clover behind the ear. She opened her eyes and smiled. "Don't get any ideas," she said. "Let's go for a swim."

"The water's too damn cold for me."

"Don't be such a big sissy," she shouted, jumped out of bed, grabbed a bar of soap, two towels and ran to the lake.

"Okay, but you go in first," Jimmy shouted as he ran after her.

Clover stopped just short of the water's edge. Jimmy 's momentum carried him into the water.

"I sure fooled you," she shouted and slowly walked into the water and dove towards Jimmy and stood up in front of him. The small beads of water on her body glistened in the sun. Her long black hair parted in the middle and lay plastered on her face. He forgot all about the cold and embraced her. "I love you, Clover."

"I love you too."

She washed her hair, and then threw the soap to Jimmy. "How about soaping me, handsome."

The two clean and refreshed bathers returned to the cottage.

"Hey, sweetheart, it's time to make plans," Jimmy said

"Lets keep them a secret for about ten minutes." Clover than took his hand and led him to the bedroom.

The sun was setting when Jimmy sat up and lit a cigarette. He leaned back against the headboard and looked at Clover "What do you think we should do?"

Clover stretched, yawned and sat up. "Remember when you told me what Albert said?"

"Yeah."

"Well, I went to a bank in Windsor and asked them if they knew of any banks in Santa Fe and they gave me a phone number."

"And?"

I called it and talked to the banker. I told him I had 2 bars of gold to sell. All he said was they deal in gold."

"Yeah, guess they won't commit themselves," Jimmy said.

"I took a chance and told them the gold was stolen. They wanted to know where from, so I told them the Canadian Mint.

Jimmy got out of bed, lit a cigarette and sat on a chair. "I don't like this."

"They knew about it. They said they were open for business so I told him my name was Clover and I'd be paying him a visit."

"When?"

"I told him three or four days. He gave me his address."

"Can't we find a place closer?"

"Dammit, Jimmy. I have no idea where else we can sell the gold. There's only one way. We have to deliver it. I have a plan, now listen to me."

"Don't I always?"

"We cross the border at Windsor, drive to Santa Fe, sell the gold, ditch the car and cross the border over into Mexico."

"Going through Windsor is way too dangerous."

"I can't run out on Bogart. I'll have to thank him for all he's done for me, and say goodbye to Belle." Clover looked long and hard at Jimmy, "I have to do it. We'll stay in a motel just out of town; make a quick stop at Bogart's in the morning, than drive. Besides, I left the bank address and phone number in the safe in Bogart's office."

"No sir, over my dead body."

"There's no other way."

"Nope."

"Jimmy!"

"Yeah, okay. But don't say I didn't warn you." Damn, why do women always get their own way?

"I have something to tell you. It's going to come as a shock," Jimmy said.

Clover looked at him with a puzzled look.

"Audrey paid me a visit the night before last. She thought I got the gold back some way or other. She wanted it and threatened me with a gun."

"What...that's hard to believe." Clover got out of bed and put her bathrobe on.

"I know."

"I didn't think she was capable of that." Clover said, "I thought she was a young woman who was wronged by the men in her life. I feel sorry for her."

"I convinced her I didn't have the gold. I'm sure she wouldn't have gone through with shooting me. That's not all. She killed Ray."

"What, oh my god," Clover said and stared at Jimmy. "Why?"

"He talked her into guiding him up here from Windsor to recover the gold then dropped her like a hot bag of popcorn when they got back."

Clover's face had a haunted look and her lower lip trembled. "Did you notify the police?"

"No. We're part of this whole mess. The last thing in the world we want is to have the cops snooping around."

"For crying out loud, Jimmy. This has gone too far."

"I offered to help her. She's a bit unhinged and walks around town looking lost and bewildered. Her parents are hoping to send her to nursing school.

"Oh, the poor soul. Even with what she did, I feel for her. She didn't deserve that treatment from Ray. But this is murder."

They walked out to the front porch staring at the lake, each lost in their own thoughts.

Clover's white pallor gave her the appearance of a statue. She couldn't stop twirling her hair with her shaking fingers as she began pacing up and down the deck. "We're in over our heads."

"We have to see this through, Clover."

"I know. There's no choice. I need a couple of days rest before we drive to Santa Fe."

"Okay, sweetheart. As long as you want." He walked down the lake, picked up stones and skipped them across the water.

His thoughts turned to his mother. When would he see her again? Except for Clover, his mother was all he had in the world. He loved his mother, but stay in Wishart Falls? He had to leave and the sooner the better.

They went to bed early. He held Clover in his arms and felt her relax and fall asleep.

They rose when the sun came over the horizon. The only sound was the birds singing and the long whistle of a freight train. Jimmy started a fire in the stove, made coffee, and then mixed pancake batter. He looked over at Clover. She came out of the bathroom and put the griddle on the stove. He could start every day like this. She was more than he deserved and ever hoped for. Maybe this Great Manitou of hers was everything she said he was. There was something he couldn't figure out. She didn't seem to want riches or fame, yet she wasn't the sweet innocent woman that left Winnipeg looking for a better life, a life where she could grow and accomplish things. Or was she?

After a swim they returned to the cottage, dressed, packed a few cooking utensils, bread, salt and pepper. Jimmy went to a small clearing behind the cottage, dug among the abandoned plants and grass and dug up worms and put them in a pail. He stopped at the shed for two fishing poles and paddles, then walked down to the lake. He turned over the canoe and put it in the water. Clover sat in the bow. Jimmy shoved the canoe out and jumped in.

They paddled in unison over the calm water to a rocky cliff at the far end of the lake. They baited their lines with worms and still fished, quickly catching three pickerel. They paddled further up the lake and turned into a narrow river than ran through lily pads, around boulders, tree stumps and over a beaver dam, until they arrived at a small grassy clearing surrounded by silver birch and aspens. Daisies and buttercups kicked up their heels in the light breeze and a few blueberries bushes still flourished. The fish sizzled in a fry pan over a campfire until they were golden brown, and then were served with bread, butter and tea. They sat in the shade of a pine tree and Jimmy played the mouth organ that he found in a dresser drawer with some of his long ago treasures. Clover sang the words from a Patsy Cline hit,

I fall to pieces each time I see you again.
I fall to pieces
How can I be just a friend?

Jimmy laughed, lay back and kicked his heels in the air.

"Let's stay for awhile," Clover said, her face beaming. "We need time together."

"It's too dangerous. Riley's not going to stop looking for us. The sooner we go, the better."

"Is this the way things will always be? Forever on the run?" Clover said as she picked up the dishes and walked to the lake and rinsed them. Jimmy followed her with the tea pail for water to extinguish the campfire. A cloud covered the sun as they packed their utensils and carried them down to the lake.

Jimmy shoved the canoe out on the water's edge, picked up a paddle and waited for Clover to get in. He had nothing to say. Clover stared straight ahead, paddled quickly then suddenly stopped, put the paddle down and crossed her arms. It was a silent trip back.

The rain came just as they landed. Jimmy picked up their gear, turned over the canoe and followed Clover into the cottage.

Jimmy walked over and put his arms around Clover. She broke away and ran into the bedroom and shut the door. "I'm sorry, we have to leave tomorrow," he shouted, sat down and lit a cigarette.

The rain stopped and the clouds disappeared. The sun was almost on the horizon when Jimmy knocked on the bedroom door.

"Come in."

Jimmy opened the door and walked in.

"I know you're right, Jimmy. It's just that I'm so tired of this." Her eyes were red. She moved over and made room for him on the bed.

"Stick with me, Clover. Some day you'll be wearing diamonds."

"Oh, just shut up," she said, and opened her arms.

"We're leaving tomorrow morning," Jimmy said.

Jimmy got up at daybreak, quietly got dressed, made coffee, poured a cup and went outside and sat on the porch steps. His mother kept saying what a nice girl Clover was. Better than he had any right to hope for. Translation: marry her before she finds out what you're really like. Then his mother started nagging him about a haircut and a new shirt, and, yep, three days and it was time to go. Can't she see he tried to be the son she hoped for? The kid who worshiped his silent and depressed father and felt loss when he died?

Clover was up, dressed and drinking coffee when Jimmy went back into the house. Two bowls of Kellogg's cornflakes and toast were sitting on the table. They ate and packed their suitcases. Jimmy shoved the canvas bag under the passenger seat and the luggage in the rumble seat. They had one stop to make.

Tears were running down Mrs. Delaney's face as she scooped ice cream into a cone and handed it to a small girl, who quickly ran from the store.

"Please, Jimmy, don't leave. You and Clover can make a life here."

"I'm sorry, Ma. I've been a failure; at least that's what you told me time and time again. I'm going to prove you wrong."

Mrs. Delaney sat sobbing. "I'm sorry, Jimmy."

Clover put her hand on Mrs. Delaney's shoulder. "Your son will be back to visit, I'll see to that."

Jimmy embraced his mother, turned and walked out the door.

The sunlight filtered though the tree leaves, bounced around on Jimmy's face and covered the tears. Was this the last time he would see his mother? Clover seemed to sense his sadness and took Jimmy's hand and led him to the car. He ran back to his mother standing in the doorway of the store, hugged her, returned to the car and sat in the passenger seat.

Red, yellow and gold leaves on the trees, the rusty brown grass and blue sky welcomed them along the gravel highway. The slight chill in the air left as they drove further south.

They stopped and parked, on North Bay's main street, in front of the Empire Hotel and went in for lunch. It wasn't the wild and noisy place where Clover stopped during the mining convention.

"I can get used to this high living," Clover said.

"So could I, but it's not me."

"Me either. I'm torn Jimmy, sometimes I want to be a schoolteacher and other times get married and raise a family."

"Whatever you want, sweetheart. I know what would make my mother happy."

The waiter brought their orders. Jimmy had a shrimp cocktail, hot beef sandwich and tea; Clover had the chicken salad and a banana split.

They held hands and walked to the car. Jimmy drove and as he passed the train station he thought of the robbery. It seemed like a long time ago.

"I can travel like this forever," Clover said.

"Good, Santa Fe isn't forever, But, it's close."

CHAPTER 23

The neon sign of the small motel, on the outskirts of Windsor, was blinking and two of the letters were out. Jimmy drove in and parked in front of the Hol ywo d Motel. The sun had just gone down and stars were appearing. Jimmy checked in, then parked the car in front of an end unit and brought in the gold and the luggage.

"This is one crummy motel," Clover said as she came out of the bathroom. "There's not enough towels, you can see through the ones they have and the bed looks dirty."

"Jesus, Clover. We have to lay low and stay out of sight. You're the one that wanted to go through Windsor. That no-good Riley has connections all over the place, we don't want to meet up with him or those Detroit bastards."

"Dammit, Jimmy, you know we have to go this way."

"Yeah, okay sweetie."

"Don't you sweetie me."

What in hell's the use, Jimmy thought. We've come this far, No sense in stirring up a nest full of trouble. We're in enough now.

"First thing in the morning we'll eat, gas up and head straight for Bogart's," he said.

Jimmy lay awake in the darkness and listened to Clover breathing as he tossed and turned. His mind wandered back to his youth, when his father would wake him up at daybreak and have a breakfast of scrambled eggs and bacon on the table, get their fishing poles out of the shed and walk down to the lake and out onto the railroad tracks to the wooden bridge. Would he ever do this with his son or be forever on the run.

Jimmy was awakened by a kiss. He watched Clover jump out of bed, open the drapes and run to the bathroom.

"Get up, lazy bones," she hollered.

Jimmy sat up and looked at his watch: eight o'clock. He lit a cigarette, looked out of the window at a wet and cloudy day. They dressed quietly and walked out to the attached restaurant for breakfast.

"I'll drive, Jimmy. You look like a guy who went three rounds with Joe Louis."

Jimmy took her hand, "That's the way I feel, I can handle it as long as you're at my side, sweetheart."

"Oh Jimmy, you're just saying that."

They returned to the room, loaded the car with their luggage and the gold; checked out and drove away.

They parked on a side street, walked to Bogart's basement office and knocked. No answer so they went around to the front door.

"Oh, thank God," Belle said when she opened the door. Her face was puffy, hair uncombed and tear-stained cheeks. Her voice wavered.

"You don't have to tell me," Clover said. "It's Bogart."

"Yes. He's back on the sauce again, and gone for the past two days. I've searched all over town for him. He never was a strong boy and so much like his father, another poor soul who drank himself to death.

"Any idea where he hung out when he was drinking?" Clover said.

Another screw up, Jimmy thought. Let's just get out of town.

"Oh, everywhere, but one of his favorite spots was the Mill Street Tavern. I've already been there twice."

"Okay, we'll go and look for him and, hopefully, bring him home," Clover said.

The smell of stale beer and cigarettes in the Mill Street tavern, along with the dark gloomy room, seemed to match the signs of hopelessness of the few patrons sitting quietly, mostly by themselves, lost in another world. Sitting over by the far wall was Bogart. His head was down on his crossed arms on the table.

"Bogart, wake up. Get your ass in gear. We're taking you home," Jimmy said and shook Bogart's shoulder. He turned and swore.

Jimmy took Bogart by the arm and pulled him up.

"We're taking you home," said Clover.

Bogart swung around, stumbled and sat down. "Leave me alone. Mind your own business." Jimmy took his arm and gently led him out into the car. Opening all the windows to get rid of the smell of vomit, stale booze and nicotine, they propped him up in the back seat, and drove him home.

Jimmy put his arm under Bogart's and led him into the house. Belle had washed her face and combed her hair. Her look of anguish and despair was gone. She was back in control as usual. "Please lay him on his bed," she said, and guided them into the bedroom. "He'll sleep it off." Bogart fell on the bed and moaned. Belle went out to the kitchen and returned with a pail and put it beside the bed.

"I'm so thankful for what you have done. He's all I have in the world," Belle said. "I thought the drinking was over."

"Let's hope it is, this time. We'll be back in the morning, Belle," Clover said.

"Oh, please do. He won't listen to me."

"Let's check in at a motel. Don't forget, I'm still working for Bogart," Clover said when they left the house.

"What in hell can we do? It's all up to him. We can't hang around."

"I can't leave, Bogart's still part of the investigation into Ray and Albert's murder. I don't want to end up a fugitive and never be able to come back to Canada. My parents are here and this is the country I want to live and die in."

"Me too, Clover. But we can end up dying sooner than later."

"We'll stop for groceries, go back to the motel we stayed at last night, and have a picnic."

One hell of a picnic, Jimmy thought. We'll probably end up in jail or shot.

They checked back into the motel. Jimmy sat on the bed and waited while Clover made ham sandwiches, poured two glasses of milk and opened a box of cookies.

"I used to love picnics when I was a little girl."

Jimmy chewed on a cookie and didn't say a word.

After they had eaten, they walked down an old road behind the motel to a small lake and sat on a couple of tree trunks, listened to the birds and watched a hawk riding thermals in the sky. A small flock of ducks circled and landed in the lake. Their squawking disturbed the peace and tranquility until they eventually settled down. Jimmy looked at Clover as she walked to the water's edge, remove her shoes and move out in the water to her knees. She turned and smiled at him. He knew Clover would be in his heart forever.

They returned to the motel room. Jimmy ate a ham sandwich and finished off the remaining cookies. He looked at Clover, smiled and said, "There's nothing like a picnic."

She closed the drapes and they both lay down and napped.

Jimmy woke up and looked around the room. Clover was sitting in a chair by the window staring out at the traffic streaming by. "Let's go to the movies," he said. "This is going to be a boring evening."

"We better not. We don't want to be noticed. I have a better idea." She undressed and lay down beside him. Jimmy felt at peace, he didn't think of the gold, his mother or the journey ahead.

They rose early, hungry and in a hurry to start their journey. The sun appeared to be cut in half by a big smokestack, as it rose above a factory roof, when they left the motel and turned onto Riverside Drive. A mixture of orange and green smog from high smokestacks on Zug Island rose in the sky. There was a smell of burnt metal and coal fumes. Two long heavy-loaded freighters slowly moved east on the Detroit River.

They parked two blocks away from Bogart's house, quickly walked to the front door, and knocked. Belle opened the door with a relieved look on her face. "Come in. I hope you haven't eaten yet. I'll make us an omelet."

"That'll be great. I'm hungry as hell," Jimmy lied.

Bogart sat on the couch, drinking coffee, and his nicotine stained fingers held a cigarette. He had a four-day growth of whiskers, disheveled hair, bloodshot eyes stained with tears. He looked down, and then covered his face with his hands. There still was a sense of defiance: as if to say, don't judge me.

Clover finally broke the ice after a long pause, "We're going away, Bogart. I came back to say goodbye. I enjoyed working for you and want to thank you. I have a few things in my desk that I'd like to take."

His glazed eyes stared at nothing in particular. "I appreciate everything you've done for me, Clover. Hopefully, tomorrow will be a better day."

"It can be, Bogart, it's all up to you," Clover said as she drank the rest of her coffee.

"I still owe you. I'll mail you a payment as soon as we get settled," Jimmy said.

"Mother, please give Clover the key." Bogart rose from the couch and walked into his bedroom.

"I know you two have a great future ahead of you. Take care of each other," Belle said while she hugged Clover. She turned to Jimmy and shook his hand.

"Jimmy, how far do you trust our police friend O'Connor?" Clover said, as she settled into her chair in Bogart's office.

"I don't like the big asshole but I think he's as honest as a cop can be in this town. He breaks the rules to accomplish what he wants. You know as well as I do, this is a corrupt city from the Mayor on down."

"We need information, Jimmy. We're going to have to make a tradeoff."

"What in hell do you mean?"

"He's investigating Ray's murder and we know who the murderer is."

"No damn way, I haven't learned much in my criminal career, but what I do know, you never squeal. That's the code Albert pounded into our heads. We spent many a day in the yard at the slammer talking about what he called ethics: you never look down on anyone, be polite, keep your nose clean and never ever give information to the cops."

"Audrey is a killer. She killed your good friend, Ray."

"I loved Ray like a brother, but don't forget he tried to take my half of the gold. He used Audrey to find my cottage to get it, then dumped her."

"Don't you forget, Jimmy, you're a suspect in Ray's murder."

"No, not really. I had a talk with Sergeant O'Connor. He has such a poor opinion of me; he doesn't figure I have the guts to kill anyone. Well, he's right on that score."

Clover frowned as she opened the safe. "Papers are spread all over." She stopped for a moment and took a few deep breaths, and frantically pulled papers out. "Oh, here it is."

"Good."

"Yeah, it's not only the address of the bank but the private phone number of the banker." She picked up the sheet of paper and put it in her purse, then picked up the phone and dialed the police station.

Jimmy paced the floor. "We have to get moving, Clover. Every minute we waste puts us in more danger."

She hung up the phone, "I just talked to O'Connor. He's on his way over. We have to talk to him."

"Well, I don't."

"Trust me. We have to clear this up before we go."

"Well, well, if it isn't my two favorite people, a private dick and a half-assed criminal. There stood Sergeant O'Connor, all six foot two of grizzle and attitude as he walked downstairs and into the office without knocking.

Jimmy felt like telling him to get the hell out. He looked at Clover. She sat back in the chair and smiled. "Hello, Sergeant, how is my favorite police officer today? We're as frustrated as you. I've been hired to try and solve this case."

"Doesn't look like you made any headway." He opened his suit jacket and hooked his fingers into his braces.

"Let's work together. Two heads are better than one. We have information that may help," Clover said.

O'Connor seemed to relax and sat down in Bogart's chair. Maybe he was starting to mellow in his old age.

"Jimmy has something to tell you." Clover said.

What in hell is she talking about; she knows damn well he'd never turn Audrey in.

O'Connor got up from the chair, adjusted his hat and looked down at Jimmy. "Don't bother. Whatever you have to say, I don't want to hear it. In fact, I don't want you stirring up a mess we'd have to fix. We're going to pin the murder on Riley and his underlings, anyway. We want to get them off the street. We have a witness who's willing to testify that Riley had a meeting with Ray Baxter the night before he was murdered. We can't nail them for killing Albert, but it won't matter. We can't hang them twice."

"Ginger is going to testify? You know damn well the mob will be after her," Jimmy said.

"It's her call, Jimmy, and I'll keep an eye on her and, besides, she insists. Now I insist you get out of town," O'Connor walked towards the door, turned and looked at Jimmy. "Don't blow it all. Save some for your future."

As O'Connor left, Jimmy glanced over at Clover "What in hell does he mean by that?"

"Figure it out for yourself."

"It's too damn dangerous here. We're going to Santa Fe to sell this gold," Jimmy said, "and we're leaving now."

Clover looked at Jimmy in a new light. He had taken charge.

CHAPTER 24

"It's an easy drive: Highway 12 Detroit to Chicago then Route 66 to Santa Fe. What's that song, Jimmy?" Clover started to sing.

Roaming free as the breeze.
Nothing to stop us and why, I can live as I please open road,
open sky.

"Something like that," Jimmy said. "We have to get moving; every minute we hang around Windsor the more dangerous it is. We have shit-head Riley with his goons on our tail, and every other son-of-a-bitch who knows about the gold. Let's fill up the tank, check the oil and get out of town."

They left Bogart's office and walked out to the car. Jimmy took the wheel of Clover's Ford coupe while she entered the passenger side, studied the road map, and turned on the radio.

The tires were bald, there was a knock in one of the cylinders and the coupe had more miles on it than a forty-year-old chorus girl in a burlesque show. Could they make it to Santa Fe?

Leaving Windsor wouldn't be easy for Jimmy. He remembered getting off the bus with Audrey, both full of hope. They were going to catch the brass ring. They lost their innocence soon enough. This was Windsor, a city, not a small village where you knew everyone. In this postwar world it was every man for himself.

He soon fell in love with the action: movies, where he could lose himself in a world of riches and thrills. Gangsters wore suits and ties and beautiful broads clung to their arms. Cowboys rode into town on white horses to bring law and order to the lawless west. Restaurants and bars on almost every street. He loved going to Detroit to drink beer, cheer the Detroit Tigers, boo the Red Wings and watch the strippers at the burlesque show.

That took money. Jimmy couldn't earn enough working in the factories that lined Walker Road. The fatigue and never-ending boredom, at his job soldering automobile radiators, was hard to take. There was an easier way to make money but it also took a toll. Robbery brought the two jail terms. One last shot at a big score was successful: a pot of gold at the end of the rainbow. Was it worth it? Ray, his partner in crime, and old Albert who taught him to survive the harsh realities of life in jail were both dead. Audrey, his old girlfriend from his hometown, who had left with him seeking a better life, was a walking ghost. He and Clover were on the run with bad guys on their tail.

They walked out of Bogart's office and climbed into the car. Hopefully this would be their final journey to Shangri-La.

The late afternoon sun sent shadows of the buildings across the quiet streets. The grey-blue sky, with huge billowing purple clouds building up in the west, seemed to indicate snow was on its way and so were they.

"Hello, folks, you look like a young couple going on a honeymoon." a customs officer said, as they stopped at the U.S. border in Detroit. He leaned down with a big smile, smelling of shaving lotion and attitude.

"Ah... just going to visit relatives in Chicago for a few days," Jimmy said. He'd never felt so nervous in his life. His face felt flushed and sweat ran down his forehead.

"Pull over to the right in front of that office door. Just a routine check," the officer said.

Jimmy waited until the customs officer was out of range, turned to Clover and said, "I couldn't help shaking, and the thought of the gold under the seat got to me."

"Let's get out of the car. Hand me the keys, I'll do the talking," Clover said in a whisper, even though there was no one around.

A different customs officer left the office and swaggered over. He was a heavy-set guy who needed a hair cut. "Well, what have we here? Let's hear your story."

"We're not married and going on a trip together. No one knows except you," Clover said. Jimmy watched as she batted her eyes at the man and looked as innocent as a teenager on her first date. How in hell did she do that?

"Well now. I can understand why this young man looks so nervous. I would be too. Sorry, folks, but I gotta follow the book. And the book says I have to look over your belongings."

Jimmy's heart was pounding as he stood beside Clover. He watched the slow methodical removal of the clothing and personal effects from the two suitcases and the search of the rumble seat and glove box. Was this the way things were going to end?

When the officer opened the door on the driver side, and bent down to look under the seat, Clover shrieked, threw her arms round Jimmy and planted a hard kiss, moving her hips against him. Jimmy just about fell over. This got the border guy's attention and his eyes almost popped out of his head. "Looks like I better let you two get on your way." He looked kind of hot and bothered, and had a silly grin on his face, as they got back into the car. Jimmy was so stunned he almost stripped the gears driving away.

"Give me a cigarette, Jimmy."

"Why? You're not going to start smoking now."

" Dammit, Jimmy. Just give me a cigarette."

"Nothing can stop us now, baby," Jimmy shouted, after they pulled away, trying to figure why she was reaching down throwing tobacco under her seat.

"Remind me to tell you the story of the Memiguiese one of these days."

"A what?"

"Tobacco is one of the scared medicines we use to give thanks for the gifts the Creator has given us."

"There's more?"

"Yes: sage, cedar and sweet grass."

"Well, I'll be go to hell."

"And another thing. Don't call me baby." She put her head on his shoulder and closed her eyes.

Jimmy settled in behind a truck travelling about fifty and relaxed as the hours went by.

Dark clouds suddenly appeared and flashes of lightning could be seen in the distance.

"We just passed a park with a sign saying cabins for rent. Let's turn around; we'll spend the night there, and you look tired," Clover said. "Besides I hate thunderstorms."

They pulled into a side street, made a U turn, drove back and turned at an open gate and into the yard. *CABINS FIVE DOLLARS A NIGHT* was written in black paint on a white painted board and nailed to a tree.

A few chimes of a bell sounded when Jimmy opened the office door. A teenaged girl sitting on a chair behind the counter, looked up from a comic book she was reading.

"We'd like a cabin for the night," Jimmy said and handed her a five-dollar bill. "She handed him a key. "Put it in the mailbox, just outside the office, when you leave. The parking lot is full, there's a spot over behind the shed."

The thunder and lightning was getting closer and the rain pelted down heavily when Jimmy started for his second trip to the car for the gold. "I'm soaked to the ass and hungry," he said when he returned and shoved the canvas bag under the bed.

"I can't do much for your hunger. Get those wet clothes off and jump in bed. I sure as hell can warm you up," Clover said. Her cheeks reddened and her eyes had a glassy look. Jimmy soon forgot his hunger as Clover led him to the bed, reached up and lifted off his wet shirt, then pushed him gently down onto the bed and knelt down before him. Later the rumbling of the far-away thunder and faint lightening flashes lulled them to sleep.

CHAPTER 25

They drove about a hundred yards back and behind two cars. Marvin and Henry had no trouble tailing Jimmy and Clover. Couple of amateurs, Marvin thought.

"Look at it this way, Henry, we have a job to do and we better not screw up. You know what Riley said."

"Yeah, I know. The dumb bastard thinks we're dumb."

They'd followed Jimmy and Clover from Windsor with strict instructions from the mob boss, Riley. They had to get their hands on the gold and bring it back. It was a long drive to Santa Fe. The sooner they got to the gold the better.

"Jesus, do you have to smoke so much?" Henry frowned and waved his arm. "My eyes are sore as hell. It bothers my driving."

"If you're so damn fussy adjust the side window. Smoking helps me think. I'm the one that has to be on the ball trying to keep Clover's car in sight and tell you what to do."

"I don't need you. I've been a driver for the mob for a hell of a long time."

" Anyway, I have a plan."

With a glance at Marvin, Henry perked up. "What's your plan?"

"Why should we turn the gold over to Riley? I say let's head to California. I heard there's a lot of action there."

"First of all, we gotta get the gold. Then what do we do with it?" asked Henry.

"We sell it someway or other. Jesus, Henry, I've never seen such a worrywart."

"I dunno, the mob has long arms. There's a guy named Mickey Cohn out there they can call. If they ever find us, you can kiss your ass goodbye."

"They just turned into a White Spot," Marvin shouted. "Guess they're going to eat"

"That's what people usually do there."

"Circle the block and pull up in the far corner of the parking lot. We'll nail them when they come out...and don't be such a wisenheimer."

Just as they turned the corner they spotted a beer truck stopped in the middle of the street; two guys were slowly running barrels down a chute and across the sidewalk into a tavern. Drivers of the blocked cars behind them leaned on their horn.

"Of all the goddamn luck, we're going to lose them," Marvin shouted.

"The tavern needs that beer. Just think if you were living around here."

"Shut up, Henry."

By the time they drove around the block and pulled in, Jimmy and Clover had left.

"Run in and get a couple of burgers and sodas. We'll catch them on the highway. They're not driving all that fast," Marvin muttered. "We gotta eat too."

They ate as they drove along, then threw the empty paper bags out of the window and relaxed.

"I felt bad about shooting Albert. I liked him. He was one of us," said Marvin.

"How in hell would we know that Albert figured they were going to a bank in Santa Fe to sell the gold? You couldn't let him live after he told us. He'd have run and told Jimmy."

"I promised to let him go if he told." Marvin sighed and stared out of the window.

"Yeah, well, Riley told you to kill him. You had to do it." Henry was nothing but supportive.

"That doesn't make me feel any better. I swear, Riley's going to get his, one of these days."

"Do you think we're going to hell when we die?"

"Not if we ask for forgiveness. Didn't you pay attention in Sunday school? Sometimes I wonder what the sisters taught you."

"I wasn't in school very long. When I was in grade seven, I was already sixteen, they more or less kicked me out." Henry's eyes were melancholy and his jaw clenched. He looked up in the sky at the threatening storm clouds, and then glanced at Marvin with a big grin. "Don't matter anyway. Spent most of my time on State Street snatching purses as people headed to Briggs Stadium for the baseball game, or robbing old guys as they sat drunk on the sidewalk. Don't forget, I almost won the Golden Gloves."

""Dammit, Henry, you didn't even qualify. I went to that boxing match."

"Well, who cares, at least I had a shot at it. When I was eighteen I teamed up with some older guys and robbed a bank; my reputation was made. Spent a little time in Wayne County jail, but it wasn't all that bad. Made a few connections."

"My old man worked at Ford's," Marvin said. "Pay was good and they were able to send me to college. Can you believe I wanted to be a bookkeeper? When Henry Ford's goons killed my dad during a strike, I had to go to work to support my mother." Marvin pounded the steering wheel with his fist, and continued. "Working in a grocery store was boring and didn't pay much. I started taking stuff home. Got caught and was fired. After running errands for the local bad guys, I kept getting bigger jobs and making lots of dough. Only thing I can't take is the look in my mother's eyes whenever I see her. But what in hell did she expect? How else is a guy going to make a good living?"

"Look at it this way, Marv, our life of crime kept us out of the army. Lot of guys I hung around with are dead, wounded or all fucked up."

"How many times have I told you the name is Marvin?"

"Okay…Marvin."

"Quick, find a place to turn around. That was Clover's car that we just met."

"Are you sure?

Where in hell are they going? They must have spotted those cabins back there," Marvin shouted. "Don't lose them. Turn around the first chance you get." Henry noticed a mailbox on a post. He turned into the driveway, waited until two cars went by, backed out and followed Clover.

"Damn, we lost them. Slow down, Henry, they're around somewhere. They sure as hell aren't going back to Windsor. Maybe they turned in at these cabins. Lets take a look-see." Most of them had a car parked in front of it, and none of them matched Clover's car. They entered the office, and Marvin approached the desk.

"Good evening, young lady." Marvin said casually.

"We're filled right up, mister."

"We're supposed to meet a young couple here. He's a tall drink of water and she's kind of dark with black hair."

'She studied them for a brief moment. "Nope, ain't seen nobody like that. They're mostly old folks and a couple of salesmen staying here."

"Thanks, kiddo, we'll be on our way."

"Something wrong here, they have to be around somewhere," Henry said as they entered the car. "Unless it wasn't them."

"It was them. I'd know Delaney's ugly puss anywhere. The hell with this, I know a peeler working in Chicago. We're old friends. We used to hang out when she danced in Detroit. If I can get in touch with her, it's going to be an evening you won't forget."

"Damn, Marvin. I'm all for it, but I just can't help thinking about Riley."

"Fuck Riley. Let's go and have some fun. We can catch Jimmy on the road. We know where they're going and I'm damn sure they'll travel on Route 66."

They headed toward the lit-up sky in the distance, the big city of Chicago. Driving down State Street the neon lights from the sign at the Rialto Burlesque shouted out, BLAZE STARR, Biggest Name in Burlesque.

"This is it, Henry. Pull in behind this building. Let's see if Baby's dancing tonight. She's one of the early acts. If she's free later, we'll have a party."

They parked the car, walked down an alley and knocked at the back door of the theatre. After waiting for about five minutes, Marvin slowly opened the door. One of the chorus line dancers was leaning against the wall, smoking a cigarette. "You guys better get the hell out of here, if you know what's good for you," she said, giving them a look-over.

"Relax, sweetheart. I'm looking for Baby Laberg, we're old friends."

"Okay. Give me your name. I'll tell her. Stay outside, the guard's a big guy."

"Tell her its Marvin from the motor city." She gave them a suspicious look. Marvin watched her walk back into the theatre and close the door. He leaned against a building across the alley and lit a cigarette. Henry just stood there.

Baby walked out, still in her dancing costume, with a light jacket, with the words Chicago Bulls written across the back, over her shoulders. "Marv! Jesus, you're a sight. Good to see you." She was short and a little on the heavy side, but was she stacked. She looked Marvin up and down and gave him a hug.

"Hello, Baby. Passing though and thought I'd look you up, hope we could go for a drink."

"I just finished for the night. Who's this handsome friend of yours?"

"My business partner, Henry. Would you have a friend for him? That dude likes to party and sure can keep a girl happy."

"Let's see if my roommate, Brandy, wants to go out. She dances in the chorus line. Wait out here. If she's willing, and I'm damn sure she will, we'll be out in about twenty minutes."

"It's going to be like old times," Marvin said.

"Sure is. I've missed you, honey."

The door opened after about thirty minutes and Baby stepped out wearing slacks, blouse and flat shoes. Brandy followed dressed about the same.

Brandy wasn't all that pretty, a bit on the old side, and showed a lot of wear and tear but Henry lit up like a Chinese lantern with a hundred-watt bulb. This was Henry's kind of woman.

"There's a bar just around the corner that serves the best corned beef sandwiches in the area," Baby said. "We're hungry as hell."

"Sounds great. As long as we can get a drink, we'll be happy," said Henry.

"It was a tough night, trying to please a bunch of yahoos in from the farm. I don't think our jobs are going to last all that long. Seems like these days everybody stays home to watch the damn television," Baby said.

"Oh, television won't last. There'll always be guys around who'd rather watch you beautiful ladies," Henry said.

Brandy smiled and took his hand.

The bar looked like it had fallen on hard times. The hand-carved mahogany booths needed re-staining and the cushions were faded and torn. The hardwood floors were pitted and lights were out in two of the hanging gold-plated lamps. The embossed wallpaper was stained with cigarette and cigar smoke. It still showed signs of long-ago elegance. Times had changed and not for the better.

"So what you doing in town, Marvin?" Baby said while they ordered food and drinks.

"We're on a business trip and if it pays off, we're going to sunny California."

"Never been there, maybe I can come out and visit?"

"Sure, and bring Brandy. I'm sure Henry would be anxious to see her."

They weren't paying attention. Brandy was snuggled up to Henry and he was staring into her eyes.

Baby raised her glass when the drinks arrived. "Here's to good luck, boys."

"Amen," said Marvin.

"You're right about the food, Baby," Marvin said after he polished off his meal. "It's damn good."

"Let's get a bottle and go to our apartment," Brandy said with a glance at Henry that didn't need interpretation.

Marvin bought a bottle of Jack Daniel's and a big bottle of coca cola.

The apartment was just around the corner. Marvin and Baby were arm and arm and Henry was holding Brandy's hand as they walked up to the third floor apartment. There were two bedrooms and a kitchen. Brandy turned on the radio and flipped around the dial and found station WQJ. She took Henry by the hand and led him to the middle of the small kitchen. "The Tennessee Waltz is one of my favorites, let's do it real slow."

Henry leaned over and wrapped her in his arms. "Slow is my middle name."

Marvin and Baby were doing it real slow, too, but they weren't dancing. Two drinks and three dances later they left for the bedroom. Henry and Brandy were already in the other one.

The city lights flickered through the window into the darkened kitchen. Smoke hung heavily around the ceiling. Henry's snoring drowned out the music from the radio and the revelers slept.

"My hangover's killing me, but it sure was worth it," Henry said, as they left the apartment around nine, leaving Baby and Brandy sound asleep. "That was one hell of a party."

"Yep, those broads sure like to make merry. Wait till we get to California. With all that gold, it's going to be some high living. Let's go for a beer or two to straighten out, hit the road, and catch up to Jimmy and Clover"

CHAPTER 26

Jimmy pulled the car up to the cabin door and loaded the canvas bag and suitcases. A cloudless sky and the sweet smell from a row of pine trees made Jimmy think of home. When will he ever go there again?

Jimmy glanced down at Clover leaning against his shoulder with her eyes closed. He lowered the music from the radio. He drove for an hour, than stopped in Kalamazoo.

"Wake up, Sleeping Beauty, time for breakfast."

They walked into a Dairy Queen just off the highway and sat in a booth. They watched a young couple sitting across from them, with a boy in a highchair. The father proudly sat and watched as the mother fed the baby applesauce. He gurgled and smiled when she wiped his face. Jimmy looked at Clover. He sensed a look of longing and watched the tears well up in her eyes, as she smiled at the baby.

"Let's eat up and get going," Clover said and looked longingly at the baby.

Jimmy paid the bill and followed her as she strode out and got into the driver's seat.

"Jimmy, get your hand from there," Clover said as she swatted his hand from her knee, when she was pulling out onto the highway. "I'm trying to concentrate on my driving," she sighed. "Sorry, I didn't mean to snap at you but sometimes I think we're in way over our heads."

Jimmy reluctantly took his hand off her knee. "Just leave it to me, sweetheart. I'll take care of you. You can count on old Jimmy."

"Jimmy, just shut up. I feel like being in my own world for now."

Women, could a guy ever figure them out? There was no way ever to tell what in hell was on their minds. Sometimes they were sweet as pie, other times they acted like a wounded tiger. No sense worrying about it, though, they damn well won't change.

"I'm sorry for crying the blues," Clover said. "The truth is, I'm torn inside. I wanted to be something, not a private dick working for a torn-down lawyer and running from the mob with a bunch of stolen gold."

"I'm going to be somebody," Jimmy said. "I fell into a bag of gold. Falling into things, that's the story of my life. One thing I'm glad about though, I fell for you."

"Be serious, you didn't force me into this. I did it of my own free will. I wanted a new life too. Living in a man's world is hard when a gal wants to become something, but that's no excuse. We both know it's wrong," Clover said as she shook her finger at Jimmy. "Your mother would be more disappointed in you than she is now if she knew; and mine…it would break her heart." Tears ran down Clover's cheeks. She pulled a folded-up piece of Kleenex from the sleeve of her dress, wiped her runny nose and tried not to cry.

"I won't tell my mother if you won't," Jimmy said with a half-assed grin on his face.

"You're impossible. Every time you open your mouth, you put your big foot in it."

Jimmy thought it would be better just to stop talking. After a long period of silence, he began to sing.

"Blue skies, nothing but blue skies from now on
"Nothing but blue skies do I see.
Never saw the sun shining so bright.
Never saw things going so right.
Noticing the days hurrying by.
When you're in love, my, how they fly."

"You are something else," Clover said and joined in the singing.

A new happy Clover suddenly had a troubled look cross her face. "There's that car again."

"What car?"

"A car that looks familiar."

"What kind was it?"

"I don't know. It's green and has big fins. I saw it this morning too, shortly after we left the restaurant. I'm going to try losing it when we go through Chicago."

"Maybe it's just your imagination. You were kind of upset back there."

"No. I tell you I saw that car in Windsor. I'm scared."

"The best chance we have is to go through the downtown area," Jimmy said, looking back. "We don't know the city, but it doesn't matter, we'll just keep going west."

They drove mile after mile, through slums, on streets with broken pavement, potholes and never-ending rows of dilapidated housing, which became an area of palatial homes nestled in among trees and manicured lawns. The sun was their guide as they drove through the city, then new suburb, and finally out into the country again.

"I haven't seen that car since," Clover said as she glanced in the rear view mirror. "Think we lost them."

"I've been watching too. Whoever it was couldn't track an elephant through four feet of snow."

"Look at that signboard, Jimmy."

"Welcome to Wisconsin," Jimmy shouted, pumped his fist in the air, then embraced Clover.

"I haven't seen you this happy in a long time, Jimmy. It makes me feel good. Now we'll turn south at the next well-traveled road; that should take us to Route 66."

"I hope we shook that car. I keep wondering how anyone knows where we were going." Jimmy said. "The only guy with any idea was Albert."

Clover didn't say anything, but Jimmy had an idea she was thinking the same as him: someone got through to Albert.

Fields of corn filled the horizon, peppered with small towns every thirty miles or so. Clover drove the car onto Route 66. It would take them to New Mexico, and hopefully a bright future.

"This will take is all the way to Santa Fe, Jimmy."

Jimmy stretched his arms out and yawned. "Pull over and I'll take over for awhile."

"Good. Let's drive for a couple of hours and stop for the night."

The hours went by and traffic started to thin out when Jimmy finally parked behind a two-story motel, well lit with neon lights. They checked into a room on the ground floor and carried in the gold and suitcases. Jimmy walked across the highway to a small restaurant and brought back fried chicken and beer. Clover was reading a book when he opened the door and country music was playing on the radio. He danced around the room, put the food on the desk and pulled up chairs. They ate, then sat outside on a bench and watched the sun go down. Clover went to bed. Jimmy stayed up, finished the beer and smoked cigarettes. He felt restless. Maybe Clover was right. Were they in over their heads?

The sunlight shone through the small opening between the drapes that covered the motel window, and shone on Jimmy's face. He squinted his eyes, stretched and sat up on the side of the bed. Another day had gone by. The morose feelings hadn't left, even though they were close to their goal and hopefully a great future. He swatted at the fly that was lazily circling Clover, nudged her, leaned over and kissed her on the forehead.

"Where are we?" Clover said as she turned and burrowed further under the sheet. "Give me another ten minutes."

"We're somewhere in Oklahoma. While you're finishing your beauty nap I'll run across the street to the restaurant. Any requests?" Clover's response was to cover her head with a pillow.

Jimmy's noisy return woke Clover up. She sat up against the pillows and yawned, and ran her hands through her disheveled hair.

His face was flushed and it wasn't because the coffee and donuts were too hard to carry.

"There's a Packard in the parking lot with Ontario license plates, he whispered.

"The car we have to worry about is a green Caddy with Michigan plates. That's the kind Riley's boys have. I'm not hungry," Clover said as she walked into the bathroom, "Just don't touch my coffee."

Jimmy relaxed and sat down and started to eat. "Yeah, that's the kind of wheels those Detroit boys drive. Anyway, get your sweet ass in gear, and let's get on our way."

Clover stuck out her tongue at him, "Okay Mr. Bossyboots."

CHAPTER 27

The traffic was light and Jimmy kept the speed at fifty while Clover watched him quietly. He was so good-looking. In moments like this she had to fight off an impulse to reach out and touch him. And he was a nice guy too, decent and caring. He'd never cheat on her or hit her like Eddie did. Hell, he'd almost never even raised his voice with her. She knew that, yes, Jimmy was hers forever—if she wanted him.

But did she? She couldn't imagine how her life came to this: on the run from mobsters, with a satchel full of stolen gold stashed under the seat. She didn't fool herself. There was a good chance they'd both be killed in the next few days. And if not, and when they sold the gold would they actually get away with it, what then? She didn't imagine the cops ever giving up on a case like this. Forty years from now, they might get a knock on the door and it'd be the cops with a pair of matching handcuffs.

She remembered stepping off the train in Union Station, back in the summer of 1940, back when the whole world seemed to be hers for the taking. She was wearing the clothes she'd worn since leaving home, wrinkled from sitting for three days in a day coach. Clover smiled at the young sailor. He was wearing white bell-bottom trousers, shirt and hat, carrying her suitcase in one hand and holding her hand in the other. He escorted her into Union station. He had just started to shave and was so shy he couldn't look her in the eye. She couldn't even remember his name. He was another prairie farm boy traveling to Halifax to sail ships across the Atlantic. He blushed when she gave him a kiss on the cheek and then left to continue his journey.

A recruitment officer sat in a booth inside the station to meet her and six other women arriving from the farms and small towns across the country. Most, like her, were away from home for the first time. Young, naïve, and ready for fun and adventure.

They rode a bus to Malton, a town on the outskirts of Toronto, to work in a war plant that built airplanes. The dormitory was crowded, the food was so-so, but who cared, they were doing their patriotic duty...and enjoying their freedom from home.

Life was swell, especially on Saturday night at the Palais Royale, dancing to Bert Niosi's band. She was popular and every serviceman wanted to dance with her. Live it up. No one has time to waste. There's a war on.

Eight months later the war ended. Sorry, ladies, we don't need you anymore and the men returning from the war need jobs.

Maybe it was the polished high brown leather boots and the red beret, who knew. She fell madly in love with Eddie, a paratrooper just returned from overseas. She moved in with him. He wanted to make up for lost time and she went along for the ride. When he beat her the second time, she left.

She sighed and Jimmy glanced over at her. She gave him a game smile. She'd been so in love with Eddie, maybe even hotter for him than she was for Jimmy. Yet he'd been a mistake. Maybe Jimmy was too.

The moment Jimmy walked into Bogart's office she had felt an attraction. He was dangerous and bad news, but also charming. He was tall and handsome, with dark hair and brown eyes and a devil- may-care attitude. He was also polite and kind, treating her with respect. He needed love; that was obvious. She was going to change him but maybe he had changed her. She was barely able to recognize herself lately, and the things she'd done.

"We've been on the road for two hours and you haven't said a word. What's the problem, is it me?" Jimmy said.

"To be honest, yes. Don't let it go to your head, but you're a good-looking guy. You know damn well a lot of women fall for you. Well I sure did, but it wasn't only because of that." She sat in silence, lost in thought.

"What's the other reason?"

"Can't you figure that out for yourself? You're caring and treat me like a lady." She turned and looked out of the back window "We're on the run with gold that you stole, and I'm part of it. But Jimmy, where's the future in that? This isn't like me, I was brought up to respect the law."

"Just think, Clover, we'll be on easy street if we pull this off; we'll settle down somewhere, have kids, maybe go back to Wishart Falls and run the store."

Clover turned to Jimmy, her big eyes flashing and impenetrable, like pools of India ink. "What's the use, you'll never understand. When something starts out bad, it usually stays that way."

""Give me a chance, I'll make it up to you. You'll see; everything will turn out great."

"Yeah, I heard that before."

The car gave a sudden jerk and skidded to the side. Jimmy fought to keep it going straight and slammed on the brakes. Again, the car skidded, the backside coming around to the front. The dust rose as the car jolted and rattled, finally coming to a stop on the hard sand just off the highway.

"A blowout. We're lucky. This could have been curtains."

"Oh my God, Jimmy. I thought we were goners." Clover got out of the car and sat on the running board. With a shaky hand she felt the slight bruise on her forehead, took off her bandana and let her hair fall. She put her hands on her knees and stared at the ground. Jimmy glanced at her but decided to keep quiet.

"The tire's ruined, let's hope the spare takes us the rest of the way." Jimmy opened the rumble seat, unhooked the spare and changed tires. He put the jack back in the rumble seat and left the damaged tire on the ground. He reached down and gently pulled Clover to her feet and embraced her.

The only sound was the wind and the traffic that sped by. Tears, mixed with the blowing sand and mascara ran down her cheeks. Her dress, wet with sweat, clung to her body. The blowing tumbleweed ran a race on the cracked baked clay. She held on to Jimmy and tried not to cry.

"Let's get a move on. We're almost there," Clover whispered. "I'll drive for a while."

"You okay?"

"Don't worry. I can handle my end."

"Atta girl, you're one big sweetheart."

"Oh, be quiet."

Her thoughts turned to life at her prairie home. There was peace and quiet, yet she craved adventure. She's experiencing it now.

A few hours later they pulled up to a diner, bought two hamburgers, two sodas and went outside. Sand blew around the outside picnic table and the colored awning snapped over their heads. A scrawny dog sat in front of Jimmy and wagged his tail.

"The only thing we have to worry about now is dealing with the bank." Jimmy said as he bent down, cupped his hands and lit a cigarette.

"I phoned the banker before we left Windsor. He's just as anxious as we are to make the deal," Clover shouted as the wind picked up. "The hell with this, let's finish our lunch in the car."

Jimmy threw the rest of his hamburger at the dog "Okay, hopefully this is the last crummy restaurant we ever eat in." He waited until Clover finished eating then drove away.

The restaurant was soon well behind them when they approached the foothills of the mountains that glistened from the vanishing sun that disappeared behind the horizon. The night sky lit up with the reflection from the lights of Santa Fe.

A few small homes and businesses came into view along the highway when they reached the outskirts of the city.

"There's a motel, Jimmy. Pull in. It looks like a good place to spend the night."

"Good idea. I'm tired."

Jimmy stopped the car in front of the office and checked in, then parked the car in front of their room.

" How about you run over to that diner next door and pick up a couple of sandwiches?" Clover asked.

"I'll get beer too.' He brought in the suitcases and the canvas bag, and then went over for the food.

Clover opened the windows, turned on the fan and lay spread-eagled on the bed. She watched a fly walk across the ceiling, than closed her eyes. She was asleep when Jimmy returned. He woke her up. They sat side by side on the bed and ate.

Clover ran the water in the bathtub and called Jimmy. "Jump in the tub and I'll wash your back."

"I hope you treat me like this all the time, sweetheart."

Clover laughed and jumped in the tub with him. They dried each other off, got into bed and covered with a sheet. "Just hold me, Jimmy. I'm really tired and my head's aching."

"Damn."

"Just go to sleep."

CHAPTER 28

Was he dreaming or was that a knocking sound? Jimmy opened his eyes, closed them and rolled over. He sat up in bed when he heard it again. He reached over and shook Clover's shoulder and whispered, "Wake up, do you hear that?"

Clover stirred and pulled the sheet over her head.

He shook her shoulder again, "Clover wake up. There's someone at the door."

"What?"

"There's someone at the goddamn door!"

"Who can that be?" She sat up.

"Let's be real quiet. If they make enough racket the desk clerk will call the cops. It's probably some drunk who's at the wrong door."

Then a third knock, more like a fist pounding. Jimmy got up, reached down and shoved the canvas bag further under the bed and then slowly walked in the darkness to the door and looked though the peephole.

"I can see the outline of someone," he whispered. "Jesus, I don't believe this. What the hell…what in the world's he doing here?"

"Who?"

"Bogart."

Clover heaved with a sigh of relief, turned on the light and grabbed her dress from the chair. "Tell him to hang on while we get dressed."

Jimmy put on his pants and glanced at Clover. She nodded. Jimmy slowly opened the door.

There stood Bogart, his agonized unshaven face and bleak eyes blinking in the glare of the ceiling light bulb.

"Hey Bogart, I don't know what you're doing here but come on in," Jimmy said. He jumped back and Clover put her hand to her mouth to stop a scream.

Bogart held a revolver and it was pointed at Jimmy.

"What in hell is this? Dammit Bogart, put that gun away. You crazy or something?" Jimmy shouted.

"Just give me the gold. I don't want to hurt anyone, but I will."

"Don't point the gun at us, it could go off…Why?" Clover asked.

Bogart swayed a bit, than sat on a chair, the gun still aimed at Jimmy.

"Let me get you a drink of water, Bogart. Maybe we can talk this out?" Clover asked, "or maybe a beer?"

Bogart stood up, swayed and turned the gun towards Clover. "Just give me the gold."

"Please sit down, Bogart. Tell me why you're doing this." The more Bogart talked the better their chances were. But there was one thing Jimmy was sure of; there was no way in hell Bogart was going to get his hands on the gold.

Bogart sat back down and waved the gun at them. "I need a new lease on life."

So do I, thought Jimmy.

Tears rolled down Bogart's cheeks. He continued. "I can't stand the one I'm living now. I have nightmares almost every night, my buddies lying dead, shelling for days on end. It's driving me crazy." The tears ran down his face. "Nobody gives a damn. We came home to a hero's welcome. Then everyone forgot about us."

Clover and Jimmy sat quietly as Bogart continued his rant. "It's the drinking that led to my gambling. I started up again and now I'm back in hock to the mob. Christ, Clover, can't you understand?"

"I thought you knew better than that. They almost killed you the last time," Clover said.

"Don't lecture me, my mother's done it all my life."

"Well, maybe you need it." Clover said. "How did you know we were here?"

"I saw the phone number and the address of the bank when I was looking for papers in the safe. It dawned on me. You have the gold and you're heading to Santa Fe to sell it" Bogart shook his head and sat up straight and continued. "When your car wasn't parked at your apartment when I checked in the morning I went to Jimmy's boarding house. The landlady said he checked out. I went home, packed a few things and left. I caught up to you yesterday morning and followed you."

"Clover said. "You know this isn't going to work."

"Yeah, you're all screwed up," Jimmy said. "Go home, Bogart, and after we sell the gold, we'll help you get straightened out. Whatever it takes. Did you think about your mother? She put up with your shenanigans for years."

"Leave her out of this."

"Maybe it's time to wise up. So far, everything you've done has only made life worse for you."

That seemed to ring a bell. Beads of sweat appeared on Bogart's forehead and the ashen color of his face looked grave. Clover pulled the other chair from in front of the desk and moved over and sat close to him. "Maybe it's time to ask for help."

"It's not going to work, Clover." The gun wavered in his hand. He appeared to be in Clover's control as she sat in front of him, mesmerizing him with those big caring eyes of hers.

Sensing his chance, Jimmy slowly moved behind Bogart. When Bogart leaned forward to talk, Jimmy made a leap, grabbing the gun in his right hand and putting an arm lock around Bogart's neck with the other. Bogart's struggle was short-lived. He was no match for Jimmy who outweighed him by forty pounds. He folded like a deck chair on the Boblo boat.

"Oh hell, what am I doing?" he gasped, sobbing and shaking like a hula dancer at a carnival. He stood up, swayed, collapsed on the bed and curled up like a baby. Clover walked over and pulled the covers over him. She put her trembling hands on Jimmy's shoulders." Oh Jimmy. This isn't what's supposed to happen."

"No, but it's all over now."

It's never going to be over, Jimmy. All I can see is trouble."

"Trust me, baby."

Her eyes were downcast and her face was white. She sat down on a chair.

"Bogart's going to need help, he's pretty far gone," she said.

"He tried to rob us. He held a gun on us. Dammit, Clover, there's a limit." Jimmy put the gun down on the table, picked up the overturned chair and sat on it. "We could be dead now."

"Well, thanks to you, we're not."

Jimmy got up, walked over and embraced her. "It took both of us."

They got dressed then sat silently looking through the motel window as a yellow streak of light appeared over the low buildings in the distance.

Bogart slept on the bed.

"I have a plan," Clover said.

"Lets hear it."

"We'll wait until nine o'clock, then I'll leave for the bank. You're going to have to stay with Bogart."

"Why can't we go together?" Jimmy said.

"Because we can't trust Bogart, that's why. Who knows what he'll do. Give me a three-hour start. Pay another day's rent; hopefully Bogart will stay another night. He needs rest. Take a bus to El Paso and look for me at the bus station."

"Look, Clover…" She'd been right so far; he might as well leave things alone.

"I'll ditch the car after I sell the gold."

Jimmy thought of the danger Clover would be in. Dealing with the bank while he rode the bus. "Jesus, Clover, I want to do more."

Okay, run over to the diner and get something to eat. Get extra, we'll leave some for Bogart."

Jimmy washed his face, combed his hair and looked at Bogart. "Keep the gun handy."

Except for the odd twitch or moan, Bogart slept on.

Jimmy returned with donuts and coffee. He set aside some for Bogart. "He's going to have to drink his coffee cold."

"Well, it'll probably taste better than it does now," Clover said as she picked up her cup, took a sip, and walked into the bathroom to shower and dress.

Jimmy looked at Bogart sleeping. Who knows what drives a person to do the things they do? Why in hell would he and Ray steal? Why would Clover help him sell the gold? He had no answers.

"It's time," Jimmy said, as he looked at his watch, when Clover came out of the bathroom. He reached under the bed, pulled out the canvas bag and carried it out and placed it under the passenger seat. Clover picked up her purse and suitcase and followed him out. He gave her a peck on the lips, opened the car door and watched her get behind the wheel. She reached out for his hand and gave it a squeeze.

"I can do it," she said.

Jimmy stood with his hands in his pockets and watched until the car disappeared. He thought of all the events that happened over the past year. It seemed like a long time since he and Ray had stolen the satchel full of gold at the North Bay station. Was it worth it? Ray was dead. Audrey, a shell of her former self, was living with her parents. Albert was dead, and that no-good son-of-a-bitch Riley was still parading around Windsor as if he owned it. The only real good thing that came out of it was Clover. So far so good but was she wavering? Would she stay?

Jimmy killed time smoking cigarettes and pacing the floor. Bogart slept. Finally at ten minutes to twelve he phoned for a cab, and then wrote a note.

Bogart, sorry all this happened. Please go home and try to straighten out. We will write later to see how you're doing and help in any way we can. Jimmy.

Jimmy heard the crunching of gravel and a car braking. He grabbed his suitcase, glanced at the sleeping Bogart, and headed out the door to the waiting taxi. It wasn't until they were well on their way to the station that he realized he'd left Bogart's gun back on the table. The hell with it, he wouldn't want to cross the border into Mexico packing a gun anyway.

CHAPTER 29

The National Bank of Santa Fe didn't look all that imposing: a small adobe building with chipped and faded blue walls and two small windows that showed lace curtains hanging inside. Clover set the canvas bag down, took a few deep breaths and opened the bank door. She picked it up with both hands and walked in. A bald-headed guy, with a bow tie and a striped shirt, sat behind one of two wickets, and puffed on a cigarette. He looked like a Las Vegas card dealer. A young guy, dressed in black with a red tie, sat in the other. He winked and beckoned her over.

"You gentlemen sure look dapper this morning. It must be the mountain air," Clover said, and smiled.

"It's not the air. It's all our girlfriends," Red Tie said with a hearty laugh. He probably had a few, Clover thought; he was a good-looking guy.

"I have an appointment with the owner. Would you tell him I'm here?"

"Sure, what's your name, sweetheart," the bald-headed teller asked.

"It's Clover. He'll know who I am."

"Do all you gringo's carry bags that heavy?"

"Just the ones with lots of gold."

Red Tie laughed.

Bow tie reached over and pressed a button that buzzed somewhere in a back room.

She sat down to wait. She drummed her fingers on the armrest and stared straight ahead.

"Good morning, Clover. I'm Carlos Alvarez, your friendly banker." His wide grin matched the rest of him. He damn near filled the doorway. A black suit with the jacket a little short on the arms and a red tie with a purple shirt gave him the look of a carnival barker. His eyes wavered around the room. His smile was about as fake as a rubber snake.

He picked up the canvas bag, took Clover by the arm and led her to a back office. She sat down on a chair by a desk; he placed the bag beside her and sat opposite her.

"Nice meeting you, Mr. Alvarez. I have friends waiting across the street and we're in a hurry." She hoped he didn't notice her nervousness and that she was lying like a Persian carpet in an Arabian tent.

"I don't see your friends, Clover. You wouldn't be telling stories, would you?"

"They're coming in twenty minutes if I'm not back," she said, as she looked him right in the eye and tried to control her breathing

"Please show me the gold bars, Clover. I'm sure it's duly stamped and ready for sale?"

"They're heavy as hell. A strong man like you can handle it better than me." He opened the canvas bag and took out the satchel, opened it and put the two bricks of gold on the desk. There was a gleam in his eyes and his mouth hung open as he ran his hand over the gold.

It took forever to cut the end off his cigar and get it lit. He glanced at the ceiling, then at the gold, and finally at Clover. "Well, Clover, I'm willing to offer you forty thousand."

"Just put the gold back in the bag. We had a deal. Other bankers are anxious to buy. You know damn well you'll get a lot more than that on the black market. The people behind this whole operation know what they're doing," Clover said, amazed at her candor. Could he see she was bluffing?

He appeared to be taken back and got up, walked to the window, leaned back and looked at her.

"Our original deal was for sixty thousand," Clover said.

He turned and walked into another room. The only sound was the ticking clock. What in hell is he doing? This is taking too long.

The sound of footsteps echoed from the corridor. Mr. Alvarez and another man emerged. Clover rose from the chair, quickly grabbed the satchel and reached for the two bars of gold sitting on the desk.

"Wait, Clover. This is my business partner, Mr. Torres. He wants to meet you."

"Ah ... Clover. It is a pleasure to meet the beautiful señorita who carries a bag full of gold. I admire your bravery and boldness. I can see you have the blood of my ancestors."

"Thank you Mr. Torres." Clover looked at the tall suave man with the thin moustache and swept back hair. She had a sense of trepidation; yet, she was calmed by his presence and charm.

"We are bankers, no need to fear us. Banks lend money and deal in currency. To be successful, we have to be honest." He smiled and opened a paper bag he was holding and laid out six packages of bundled bills on the desk. "Trust me, there's sixty thousand there." Clover tried not to shake, picked up a package and thumbed through the crisp new US dollar bills and counted it. She leafed through the other five packages, and then jammed them into her purse. She stood up, looked both men in the eye, said thank you and slowly walked out of the building.

Her legs moved with difficulty. They were stiff and weak. She leaned against the building for a few minutes, felt herself gain strength and started walking again.

Clover turned at the corner of the bank and walked to her car. A green Cadillac was parked behind her coupe. Her heart stopped, restarted and raced like a runaway horse. Her hand tightened on her purse, she turned and ran back into the bank.

"Clover! Good to see you again," Bow Tie shouted. "I didn't think you missed me that much."

Clover ignored him and ran towards the side door. Had those goons seen her? She looked back and saw them leave their car. She bolted across the street, weaving through moving trucks and cars, and aimed for a fruit stand on the sidewalk.

She crouched behind a table, piled high with fruit. A startled old man, with a huge moustache and wearing an apron, looked at her and raised his hands, as if to say, what in hell did you do, lady?

"Pardon me, señor. My husband's chasing me. Can you hide me? He's drunk again."

He frowned. "Go in back and run into the tent." He then turned and shouted, "Maria, shelter this young woman."

Clover ran into the tent and sat on a stool and shook like a car running on two cylinders. Maria, short and heavy, put an arm around her. Clover felt a huge relief. For some reason or other, she felt safe. She peered out, through a small tear in the tent, towards the fruit stand and shrunk back when she noticed Marvin and Henry standing there. Her heart raced even harder.

"Have you see a woman, very pretty with black hair, carrying a big purse?" Marvin asked the fruit stand owner.

"Si, a woman like that was running that way," he said and pointed down the main-street. It was bustling with people.

Clover watched as they hurriedly walked in the direction Mr. Alvarez pointed.

When they were out of sight, she breathed a sigh of relief. Turning to Maria, she asked where she could get a cab.

"Wait," Maria said. "Manuel, come quickly." They walked out of the tent that backed onto an alleyway. Maria beckoned her towards a horse hitched up to a wagon. Manuel helped her up onto the seat, jumped on and grabbed the reins. "Where can I take you?

"In front of the bank on the corner, please. I'll tell you where to stop."

The rhythm of the noise from the trotting horse brought back memories of the farm where she grew up. She thought of her father when he drove a horse and pulled a load of wheat. Hopefully, someday she will return to the prairies.

As they approached her coupe, her hand tightened on her purse, she looked both ways, and jumped down from the wagon.

"Manuel, I owe you my life. All I can do is say thank you. I'm going to leave my car near the bus station. I'll leave the keys in it. It's yours if you want it. Please tell me where the bus station is."

He looked at her with suspicion. "I cannot take your car, señora, but I thank you. Stay on this street and you will come to it."

She ran to the car, hopped in, and drove slowly until she saw the bus station. She parked a block away, left the keys in the ignition, grabbed her suitcase and hurried to the bus station.

There was a long line to the ticket counter. Clover's breathing was returning to normal as they inched ahead. She kept looking back to the door. She tucked in her blouse and adjusted her skirt with her free hand. She held the purse tightly with the other. Are people staring? Oh, God, will this journey ever end? She finally stood in front of the ticket counter. "One way to El Paso, please."

The clerk stamped the ticket and handed it to her. She put the money on the counter, he picked it up and handed her the change. "The bus leaves in thirty minutes," he said. She hurried to the washroom, washed her face and combed her hair. She stood behind a post and watched the entrance to the station until the bus arrived, than quickly boarded.

CHAPTER 30

Sunshine washed over the pavement as the Santa Fe town square shimmered, mirage like, in the distance. Marvin and Henry left the fruit stand, and walked towards the square.

A stiff breeze swirled bits of paper into the air. High above, huge clouds drifted lazily across the sky.

"Clover's given us the slip," Henry whispered. He was breathing heavily and his shirt was wet with sweat. He carried his jacket in one hand and held his side with the other. "I swear that woman is one lucky dame."

Throngs of people, young and old, were celebrating in the streets. Bands played, people sang and danced the cha-cha. Children rode the Ferris wheel and carousel. A parade had started, led by men carrying a picture of the Virgin. The whole area smelled of caramel, cooking grease and exploded firecrackers.

"Must be one of those religious holidays," Henry said. "We'll never find her around here. There's some damn fine looking señoritas around though. Want to try our luck?"

"Yeah, but not now. We'll have plenty of time for that after we get our hands on that money. Maybe that fruit seller lied to us," Marvin said between gasps. He leaned over on a lamppost and tried to catch his breath. "I'd like to go back and straighten him out but we haven't got time. Clover can't be that far ahead."

"I think that's her across the street!" Henry said. "She just went behind that refreshment stand."

Marvin quickly turned and started walking across the street. A young police officer put his arm out. "This is the parade route and it's blocked, Señor."

"We gotta cross," Marvin said.

"I will shoot you if you do, Señor."

They turned back to the sidewalk and zigzagged through the crowd in the direction of the refreshment stand and ran across the street.

"I think that's her just ahead," Henry said.

"That's not her, you dumb bastard."

"Well, it looked like her to me."

"Do you realize we could have been shot by that trigger-happy cop?" Marvin said and sat on the curb, fanning his face with his hat.

"At least, I'm trying. You're not doing a damn thing except bitch and call me names."

Marvin didn't say anything. They got up and slowly walked back to their car and kept looking around to see if Clover might still be around.

"Her car's gone!" Henry shouted as he approached their car. He unlocked and opened the two front doors and windows of the Cadillac. They waited a few minutes for the heat to pour out, entered the car and sat peering through the bug-splattered windshield.

Marvin was leaning over with his head between his hands. Henry slouched down with his elbow on the window frame and toyed with the car keys in the ignition.

"Henry, stop that fucking racket."

"Clover probably sold the gold already," Henry said. "Where do you think they went?"

"Jesus, Henry, you ask the dumbest fucking questions. How am I supposed to know?" Marvin took his hat off, pulled out his handkerchief and wiped his brow before he leaned back and lit a cigarette.

"Know what I think, Marvin?"

"I have no idea, I'm sure it's important."

"You can be damn sarcastic, can't you?"

"Okay, let's hear it."

Henry took a deep breath and leaned over. "It looks like she sold the gold. What do you think they'd do?"

"Damned if I know. You tell me."

"Here's the way I figure it. They'd probably go to Mexico and travel inland, probably go west. Maybe even spend the winter there."

"So?"

"I don't think they'd travel by car. It's dangerous traveling through the mountains with bandits all over the place and the bad weather."

"Damn, Henry. You could be right." Marvin sat up straight. "They'd travel by train. Let's fill up, hightail it to Juarez, and find the railroad station. It's worth a chance. We got nothing to lose."

"You better call Riley."

"No damn way. We're not working for him anymore. We get our hands on that money, we're going to California and never see Riley's ugly puss again."

Henry eased the Cadillac out of the parking spot and drove through the busy streets heading south.

A sudden rain shower began and cooled things off. A rainbow arced through the sunlight.

"There's a pot of gold at the end of that, Marvin."

Marvin laughed, lit a cigarette and turned to Henry. "I never did like that son-of-a-bitch."

"Who, Riley?"

"Yeah. He treated us like dirt. I heard on good authority he's on the hot seat. Unless we get the money and bring it back, he's a dead man."

"Well, he's going to be dead then. We ain't going back. I'm getting hungry. Let's find a place to eat, then drive to El Paso and across the border."

"Do you think we should? Maybe we should get the lead out. Go get these two before they give us the slip again."

Henry shook his head. "I'm hungry. If they're going to Juarez, we'll get em. Don't worry, besides I think better on a full stomach."

"Who made you the goddamn boss?"

"I'm driving."

CHAPTER 31

The taxi driver cursed as he wove his cab through the busy streets. Cars, trucks and horses were trying to maneuver between people, dogs and the odd cat. They were still a block away from the bus station and stopped behind a horse and wagon unloading produce at a small fruit stand. Jimmy paid his fare, grabbed his suitcase, got out and walked to the Santa Fe station. Everybody must be leaving town, Jimmy thought, as he jostled his way through the crowd, into the station and stood in a line. When he made it to the ticket window, he asked. "When's the next bus for El Paso?"

"One just left, Señor. The next one is due in four hours," the elderly ticket seller said, a cigarette, with about an inch of ash on it, dangling from his mouth.

"Give me a one-way ticket."

Jimmy paid, picked up the ticket and surveyed the waiting room. Sunlight streamed through the long windows and made rectangular images on the hardwood floor. A mother was passing out food to her children from a large paper bag. A young couple held hands, the girl radiant as she smiled at the boy. He looked worried. Four middle-aged men in black suits sat on a bench, staring into space. They could have been brothers.

Jimmy hurried over to an unoccupied bench. He folded his jacket for a pillow, stretched out, put his arms across his eyes and tried to sleep, but he couldn't get Clover off of his mind. She had a bee in her bonnet. It was like he told Ray; you have to grab that brass ring. The sounds of squalling babies, noisy kids and shouting mothers put him between consciousness and a dream world. He tried to fight it, but a wave of depression hit him hard. For some reason, he always ended up behind the eight ball. He didn't want a big yacht filled with beautiful babes and booze. Just to sit on the sand with Clover by his side and a glass of tequila and watch the sun go down was enough for him.

Four hours until the bloody bus comes! Clover would be kicking around El Paso thinking he must have died—if she was waiting around. Clover was the sweetest girl in the world, but she lost her innocence a long time ago, and now she had a small fortune in her hands. What did she have in mind? She was a classy dame and why would she fall for me. Would she double-cross me like Ray did? What's to stop her from turning around and going back north? Maybe she's going there now with the money. Back to her birthplace for a rest, then to any place she feels like.

Jimmy shifted around on the hard wooden bench, trying to get comfortable. It was a lost cause.

What am I? A jailbird from the sticks whose only skill is bullshit? What went wrong? My upbringing was as good as most. My parents

wanted me to grow up to be a useful citizen. When dad wasn't work-
ing he didn't get any enjoyment out of life. Ma said it was the effects
of the war; who in hell knows. Now, she was different: outgoing, talk-
ative, keeping up with the times as best she could with the Eaton cata-
logue for fashion and the Toronto Star for news. But me, I couldn't
do anything right in her eyes. Maybe for not trying and reading
too damn many comic books. Cowboys rode the west, Superman and
Batman made everything easy. Maybe I should've tried harder in
school, I don't know, maybe Ma was right. I should not have been
such an asshole and did what I was told.

Who in hell can you trust? Ray double-crossed me. Audrey, the
woman I grew up with and actually loved me killed Ray and threat-
ened to kill me for the gold.

Jimmy sat up. His neck was sore, his left leg had gone to
sleep and he had one hell of a headache.

He stood up and walked to the washroom. Paper, cigarette
butts and burnt out matchsticks were all over the floor. The
smell of urine and shit made him gag. He washed his hands
and face with a dirty bar of soap and cold water, dried them
with his handkerchief and walked outside for some fresh air.

A food vendor's call and the smell of fried onions, reminded him he hadn't eaten. He bought a taco and a beer, wandered
over to a raised platform, sat down and leaned back against a
post. The food was good and the beer was cold. He closed his
eyes and savored the moment.

CHAPTER 32

The bus almost stalled as it labored up the steep hills, then careening around corners on the way down. The noise from the engine and the whistling of the wind through the open windows combined with the smell of gasoline and engine exhaust had an affect on the passengers. Those who weren't sleeping seemed to sit in a stupor. Even the kids were quiet.

Clover sat with her eyes closed, not paying much attention to the old gentleman sitting beside her as he talked. He was going home after spending four months working on the fruit and vegetable fields in California. She was too damn tired to be polite. She pretended to sleep.

This wasn't like her. Why in hell did she fall for a guy like Jimmy? Maybe it was the excitement she felt when we they were together. He was a charming guy, well meaning, yet certainly not an ideal husband. Maybe she could redeem him. Bring back the qualities she could see in him. Deep down, though, she knew that trying to rebuild a man generally didn't work.

"I'm sorry, senõr. It was rude of me. Sometimes things get out of hand," she said, as she turned to him.

He looked at her, raised his head and touched his straw hat. "Please don't worry senõra. I can see you are having trying times. I can tell by your face. Life is strange. Sometimes I'm that way myself, but not today. Forty years traveling back and forth, leaving my family for months, has ended." After a long pause he continued. "We own our small farm and my children are all grown up. Returning to them still feels the same. It's like a new day. While I'm away, things change. Babies are born and people die. Life goes on. So far, the Virgin has smiled on me."

Clover thought back to her own family, who also toiled in the fields. The Great Manitou smiled down on them.

The tired look on his face disappeared. "That is the light from my village in the distance. My family will say a prayer for you tonight, señora. I hope that your heart soon finds the peace it's looking for." The bus pulled up, in front of the lone store in a dusty village, and stopped with what seemed to be a sigh and a shudder. The old man made the sign of the cross, rose and walked to the exit. He was a proud and happy man walking into the arms of his family.

Clover's shoulders dropped and tension in her neck disappeared. The burden she carried seemed to lift. She drifted into a peaceful sleep and dreamt of a future where a family mattered and honest law-abiding people lived.

The bus traveled on through the dusty hills and valleys and finally stopped at the crowded bus station in El Paso.

Clover sat and waited until the passengers jostled and shoved their way off the bus, then followed them into the bus station All she had to do was wait for Jimmy and hope the dumb ass wouldn't get lost. Then they would take a taxi to the train station in Juarez and travel to safety on the Gulf of California in Mexico.

Can she go through with it? Guess there was no choice now.

CHAPTER 33

Laughter, shouting and the never-ending noise of children crying, woke Jimmy up from his reverie. He was tired and sore but felt good. He quickly stood up, grabbed his suitcase and joined the group forming a lineup on the platform. The bus slowly pulled in and stopped in front of them. After what seemed forever, the incoming passengers left the bus and Jimmy climbed on.

He sat in the back of the bus, hoping to get some sleep. The bus was full. A young woman walked down the aisle, with a crying baby in her arms. He knew damn well where she would sit. With a look of resignation she looked at Jimmy put the baby down on the seat and placed her battered suitcase in the upper rack, then picked up the baby and sat down. He reached over and gently placed his hand under the baby's chin and smiled. The child quit crying, looked steadily at him for a moment and shyly grinned. A sense of peace and calm came over Jimmy. Maybe Clover was right after all. Some things were more important than others.

"Gracias, Señor," the mother said. "You are a good man. May my son turn out like you."

Jesus, Jimmy thought. What a thing to wish on a kid.

Mile after mile the bus jostled, vibrated, the engine straining on the hills as they rode through the night, stopping at small villages along the way. Jimmy slept as peacefully as the baby in his mother's arms beside him. He woke as they pulled into the El Paso bus station. He put his hands on both sides of his eyes and peered through the smeared and fly- splattered window. His could hear his heart pounding.

The bus stopped, he picked up the woman's suitcase, his own and followed her out. He set hers down and watched as a young man came forward, embraced her and the baby, picked up her suitcase and lead them to a horse and wagon.

Jimmy stood on the platform and looked at the crowd. Where was she? He began walking slowly through the milling people. Faces drifted in and out among the dim light from the lampposts. Clover should be waiting; she knew he was on the bus. He entered the station and walked between the benches searching for her. He could hear his heart beating. He walked outside onto the almost empty platform.

A figure of a woman came out of the shadows and slowly walked towards him. As she came closer, he recognized Clover. He reached for her. They embraced and clung to each other.

"Oh, Jimmy,"

Jimmy held her tight. "Oh, Clover. I thought I lost you."

"We did it, I sold the gold," she whispered. "The 60,000 dollars is in my purse."

His hands trembled. He let out a huge breath. "Clover," was all he could say.

He hugged her tighter.

"I waited and waited. I thought the bus would never come," she said.

"We have a future now." He touched the purse.

"Let's call a taxi and go to the train station," she said.

"The main thing is we're together, with 60,000 dollars," Jimmy said.

"We still have to clear the Mexican customs." As far as they're concerned, we're going to spend a few days at the races."

"Okay, hope they buy it." He couldn't stop smiling.

Jimmy flagged a taxi that was slowly cruising by. The open windows helped lower the odor of gas fumes and the acrid smell of the cheap cigar in the driver's mouth.

"Juarez train station," Jimmy said as they entered and sat apart to avoid the cushion spring protruding in the center of the seat. The loud noise of the engine and the heavy traffic combined with the jarring of the broken spring on the left back wheel added to the frustration.

"Start making plans, baby. The whole wide world is ours," Jimmy shouted.

"I can't hear you."

Jimmy leaned across and spoke louder. "I said, let's make some plans."

Clover cupped her mouth with her hands and replied, "All we have to do is give twenty percent to the shipping supervisor at the mine for his help."

"Yeah, I know. We have to call Bogart too. I hope he went the hell home. The poor bastard's in bad shape."

"I wonder where those two misfits are?" said Clover.

"Probably gone back with their tails between their legs to report to Riley. Forget about them, let's talk about our future."

"Let's just relax."

Jimmy looked at her in surprise. What happened to her exuberance? She sounded more pensive than happy as she stared out the window.

Jimmy lit up a cigarette and leaned back. His thoughts went back to the simpler times with Ray, chasing girls, speeding around town in Ray's beat-up old car pulling the odd theft. He and Ray drinking in the Temple Hotel with Albert and listening to the three-man band on stage playing country music. Even the times in jail seemed to pass quickly. If his buddy, Ray, hadn't been killed he wouldn't have met Clover. Guess you call that fate.

The clouds had lifted and a faint light of the sun was showing through the clouds and sent shadows across the Mexican customs buildings. The taxi came to a stop behind a long line of cars. The taxi driver threw his cigar out of the window, took off his cap, leaned back on the seat and closed his eyes.

"What if they search your purse?"

"Dammit, Jimmy, don't start." Clover reached over and took his hand. "Anyway, my dream catcher's on top of the money."

"Yeah, and I suppose you have some tobacco in your purse too?"

" Sometimes you're a real smart ass. I'm just as nervous and scared as you are. Just get a grip!"

Jimmy had never seen her so angry before. She was all wound up and ticking like a two-dollar watch. "Jesus, I'm sorry. I shouldn't have said that."

"I'm barely hanging on. You're sure not helping things." She began to quietly sob.

He thought of the picture of Jesus on the cross from the boarding house wall that he put in his suitcase when he left. He would see them through if Clover's dream catcher didn't.

It was late afternoon when they got to the head of the line.

"Good evening. Welcome to Mexico," the customs officer said as he bent down and looked at Jimmy. "All the gringos coming through are going to the racetrack. I bet you going there too."

"Ah…that's where we're going," Jimmy managed to say.

The customs officer looked at Clover and smiled. "Have fun, señora and fill your purse with pesos."

The taxi pulled away and headed for the Juarez train station.

"We're home free, baby." Jimmy threw his arms around her. "There's no stopping us now."

"You almost knocked me over," she snapped at him. She pushed him away. "And lower your voice."

His joy evaporated as quickly as it had come. What the hell had he done now

Sometimes it seemed like there was no pleasing women.

CHAPTER 34

Jimmy smiled as the train station came into view. He placed his hand on Clover's knee and squeezed. The long journey was almost over. The taxi pulled up in front of the waiting room, the driver pulled two suitcases from the trunk and set them down. His eyes opened wide when Jimmy paid him. "Muchas gracias Senõr. Good luck wherever you're going."

Jimmy picked up the luggage, leaned over, and nudged Clover with his shoulder. "We're here, baby. Only good things can happen now."

"I'm sorry, Jimmy." She reached over and wiped the tears from her eyes with the sleeve of her dress. "Sorry to be such a nervous Nellie. Maybe things will get better."

"You can say that again."

Jimmy laughed. He was a new man. Gone were the doubts and fears that had troubled him ever since he'd stolen the gold. He and Clover were over the border and soon they'd head away from their concerns and problems. His matted hair, stubble on his chin and wrinkled pants were the only signs of a long hard journey. His brown eyes burned with the intensity of a man focused on a future that was finally in his grasp. He had lost weight but looked like someone who had found his place in the world.

The wooden sign at the train station read Juarez, but to Jimmy it said Freedom. They'd ditched their pursuers back in the U.S. and soon he and Clover would catch a train to take them deeper into Mexico. Sure, the place wasn't as clean or cheery as Canada or the States. The people milling about on the wooden platform were poorly dressed…but to Jimmy, the Mexicans also looked strong, a no-nonsense people. He could see himself being content here, especially with the fortune Clover carried in her purse. Clover, on the other hand, seemed lost. The sparkle had left her eyes.

Jimmy studied her. She wore her favorite dress, with red, blue and white flowers, now creased and worn. She reminded him of the Madonna, although he didn't know why. What was going on in her head? Was it to follow her dream of becoming a teacher and living in the traditions of the steadfast and glorious past of her Métis heritage?

He didn't want to return to his past: running a poker joint, travelling on buses, jail time and, before that, living in the backwoods of Northern Ontario.

He stopped and set down a suitcase. Placing his arm around Clover's waist he pulled her closer and kissed her softly on the forehead. Clover looked up at him with a slight smile then looked away. He lowered his arm and pinched her on her thigh. She gave him a slight slap on the hand in return. What was on her mind? He glanced at Clover's purse with its fortune sitting under a torn dream catcher. Was this his future? He hoped it was hers.

"You look tired, sweetheart," he said.

"I am."

"You know what I'm going to do tomorrow?"

Clover smiled. "With you it could be anything."

"I'm going to buy a pair of cowboy boots and a hat, then buy you one of those shawls and a fan that señoritas carry."

"Oh, Jimmy, only you would say that."

"That's what I'll be doing from now on, taking care of you. Forever."

Clover glanced at him and lowered her eyes. Jimmy hoped it was because she was overwhelmed with relief or maybe even love.

The passenger board on the outside wall near the door had the words A Tiempo written in chalk beside the number of the train to Los Mochis. It was scheduled to leave in two hours. Jimmy and Clover approached the ticket window.

The ticket seller put his cigarette in an ashtray, looked furtively at Clover, than turned his eyes to Jimmy and asked, "Adonde?"

Jimmy bought two first class tickets to Los Mochis, then took Clover by the hand and walked outside.

"This is our world now baby: a wagon full of happiness on a downhill pull. No one knows where we are. We'll be on the Gulf of California soon."

Clover looked at him and seemed about to speak then looked away.

Jimmy peered through the station door. "It's crowded as hell in there. Let's sit on a bench outside."

"Let's go in. I have a funny feeling and I can't quit worrying."

What in hell was she worried about? He father used to say he never understood women. The old man sure was right about that. After all, the bad times were over and Clover was more worried than ever. "Okay, there must be an empty bench somewhere," he said.

They found one at the rear of the waiting room. They sat down and put their suitcases in front of them. Jimmy grinned when Clover took her shoes off, tucked her feet under her thigh, and leaned against him, holding her purse to her chest. He relaxed and crossed his arms and legs.

The women sitting around them were talking softly to each other. The men sat and smoked, staring into space.

"Are you sleeping, Clover?" he whispered.

"Not anymore."

"It's too damn boring sitting here. Let's go across the street to that little cantina. I'm hungry and need a drink."

"We have a lot at stake, Jimmy. Let's stay put and get something from the street vendor."

"Just one drink."

"You go; I'll stay here."

"Come on. We're going to be together from now on, we won't be long."

"After all that crying the blues and if it'll make you happy, okay, but let's make it snappy."

He leaned over and kissed the nape of her neck.

She shivered. "You're looking for trouble, Jimmy." She attempted a smile. "Just one drink and we're getting the hell back here. I'm nervous."

Music from a mariachi band played in the distance. They walked up the street to a cantina. Laughter and singing resonated through the open door. A few couples were dancing on a small dance floor to the music of three trumpets, a violin and a guitar. Some of the American patrons must have had a good day at the racetrack. It was one big party.

They walked in and sat at a table away from the dance floor and the band.

"Aren't you glad we came? It's time we start celebrating," Jimmy said.

"I told you, Jimmy, I'm nervous."

Jimmy lit a cigarette. Why push it. There would be plenty of time for raising hell when they settled down.

When a smiling waitress approached, Jimmy ordered two burritos and tequila. He felt he was in heaven. He sat with one hand resting on Clover's arm and the other holding his drink. Just the way he'd imagined.

Leaning over to whisper in Clover's ear, he noticed her wide-eyed stare, the pallor of her face and her open mouth. "Oh no," she said and reached for Jimmy's hand.

"What the hell?" he said.

He glanced in the direction she was looking. It couldn't be. Six tables over sat the two thugs, Marvin and Henry, grinning at them like a pair of apes in a Tarzan movie.

Eyes bleak and mouth wavering, Clover's hand tightened on her purse. She turned to Jimmy and whispered, "What are we going to do?"

Jimmy's heart raced. Flashes of fear and anger flowed. Was this how it was going to end?

The music stopped, Marvin sauntered over to their table and Henry moved to the door.

"Look what we have here," Marvin said with a sly grin. "Pretty Clover and the gold thief. Get up slowly and walk outside." He moved his hand showing it held a .38 inside his suit coat pocket, and pressed it to the side of Jimmy's head. "Move."

Jimmy rose from the chair, took Clover's hand and guided her through the tables to the door. Flashes of panic and dread coursed through him. His mind reeled with thoughts of Clover, the gold, self-preservation and his mother. Was this the end?

"Jesus, Marvin, this is getting out of hand. Look, you can have the money," Jimmy said.

Marvin laughed, "Looks like we already have it. Keep moving and follow Henry."

Jimmy's voice rose. "Let Clover go. She has nothing to do with this."

"For the last time, move."

They walked past the cantina, farther away from the train station, and veered off behind a smaller building.

Henry pulled Clover away. He put his arm around her and drew her close.

"We have ourselves a real honey here, Marvin."

Clover struggled. "Leave me alone you big goon."

Jimmy tensed and took a step towards Henry.

Marvin yelled as he jammed the barrel of the gun into Jimmy's back "Don't do it, Jimmy. Leave her alone, Henry. There'll be plenty of pretty women in California."

"Not too many like this one though. She's one sweet dame," Henry said. "Besides your days as boss are almost over. When we split the cash we're on our own."

"We've been partners for a long time, Henry."

"That was then, this is now."

"I've been carrying you. You'd be nowhere without me."

"Fuck you, Marvin," Henry said and stepped away from Clover.

They turned off and walked through a passageway that ran behind the building and under a light fixture on a large warehouse. They stopped at a wide space between two parked cars.

"How did you know we were taking the train from Juarez?" Clover asked.

"Because we're smart, that's why." Marvin smiled. "Now cut out the bullshit and hand over your purse."

"Do as he says," Jimmy said as Clover stood there and didn't move. Jimmy reached over and took the purse from her hand and held it out to Marvin. "Let us go. There's nothing we can do. We can't even go to the cops."

"Aw, sorry, Jimmy," Marvin said. He grabbed the purse. "This is the end of the line."

"Give us a break, Marvin. We can't hurt you now," Jimmy said as he put his arm around Clover.

"We don't leave witnesses."

"Hold on, Marvin," Henry said. "Let's split the money first and I'll take Clover along with it."

"Christ, Henry, What in hell is the matter with you? There's plenty of time to split the cash, and you're not getting Clover. She'll slow us down."

"No time like right now. Start counting the money." Henry moved towards Marvin, towering over him.

"What's the big rush anyway? This isn't the time. Let's wait until we get back across the border. Then we can go our separate ways," Marvin said.

"I told you. We're through when we got the dough. You've been lording it over me for a long time. That bullshit's all over."

"Okay. Why not." Marvin opened Clover's purse, and stared at the packages of bills in the bag. He pulled out a package and kissed it. The light from the hanging bulb reflected in his eyes. "Henry, we're rich." He handed two packages to Henry.

"What in hell...where did you learn to count?"

"I'm in charge, the brain, that's why. I get the bigger share."

Henry grabbed Marvin and shoved him against a parked truck. His hat flew off his head. Marvin turned away and raised his hands to protect himself but it didn't do much good. Henry hit him with his fist and knocked him to the ground.

Jimmy hesitated. Was this their chance? Make a run for it while Marvin and Henry were fighting? Jimmy didn't see them getting more than six steps, but what the hell. He grabbed Clover's hand and set himself for the dash of his life. Then he froze.

Henry pulled his pistol out of shoulder holster. He didn't bother to say anything, just fired it at Marvin. Marvin rose on his elbow then fell back, his head lolling to one side. Henry reached down, picked up the purse and rifled through it for the packages of bills.

Jimmy found himself moving. He leaped on Henry's back with one thought: he had to get the gun. It flew out of Henry's hand and landed at Clover's feet.

Henry stumbled but righted himself, shaking Jimmy off. Two 200-pound men squared off, sizing each other up, each waiting for the other to make the first move. Jimmy felt his pulse throbbing in his head. This wasn't just about the money anymore; this was about Clover.

Jimmy charged. Henry feigned and sent a shot in Jimmy's gut that knocked the wind out of him. He followed up with a punch to the side of his face. Jimmy's vision blurred and he tasted blood.

Jimmy backed up, twisting and turning and trying to avoid Henry's blows. It was obvious that Henry was an experienced fighter. Jimmy could count on one hand the bar fights he'd been in. For most of them he'd been on the losing side.

Jimmy swung his foot and caught Henry in the groin. He doubled over and Jimmy pounced. He could hear the fabric ripping when he grabbed Henry's shirt, shoved him to the ground and fell on top of him.

"You son-of-a-bitch," Henry said gasping for breath. They rolled in the dirt with arms flailing, grunting and groaning. The battle slowed. Henry put a chokehold on Jimmy and rolled on top of him. Jimmy's arm swung wild as he struggled to breath. His hands clawed the ground, searching for something, anything. One hand contacted something hard—a rock. He gripped it and swung. It glanced off the side of Henry's head hard enough to lose his grip on Jimmy.

Jimmy staggered to his feet, struggled to get his balance. He had to win: for Clover, for everything they'd gone through to get this far, for the future. He gathered up every ounce of strength he had and made a run at Henry. Henry sidestepped and swung a haymaker that connected with the side of Jimmy's head. He felt nausea and everything dimmed. He fell to the ground; his fight was over.

Henry looked down at Jimmy and began kicking him methodically. Jimmy curled into a ball and covered his head with his hands, protecting himself as best he could. From the corner of his eye he caught a glimpse of Clover. She had the gun in both hands and pointed at Henry.

A shot rang out and Henry fell over. The sound came from somewhere behind Jimmy. He turned. Marvin. A gun fell from his hand and he slowly sank back to the ground.

Clover rushed over, took Jimmy's arm and helped him up. He swayed and put his arm around Clover for support.

"Hurry," Clover shouted.

Jimmy gasped for breath. He looked at the two lifeless bodies. "The money...we have to get the money."

Clover reached down. Picked up her purse and the two bundles of bills from the ground.

She leaned against the truck. Her voice broke, "I almost killed—"

"You were going to save my life and your own," Jimmy said, his breathing, hoarse and raspy. "We have to get out of here." He took a step forward, reeled and fell to his knees. "Clover..."

She grabbed his arm and helped him up.

He fell again, pulled himself up on one knee and reached his hand to Clover.

She took it and helped him rise from the ground. He stumbled along behind her.

The mariachi band was still playing when they approached the cantina. They stopped. Clover dusted Jimmy's suit with her hands. "Run in and wash your face and hands. You're a sight. Stop at our table and get my suitcase."

"Why? There's nothing in it we can't replace."

"I want my suitcase. I need my things."

Jimmy limped into the cantina. The small dance floor was full of people dancing, throbbing to the music and groups were singing at the tables. It was Jimmy's kind of party, only he wasn't in the mood. When he got to the men's room, the reflection in the mirror frightened him. One eye, black and yellow, was swollen shut and his face was scratched and covered with dirt and blood. He opened the water tap and tenderly wiped his face with his handkerchief, dusted the sand off his head and combed his hair. Then he forced himself to saunter over to the table where they had been sitting and picked up their suitcases. He ordered a double shot of tequila at the bar, swigged it down. Then he walked out the door.

Clover was waiting in the shadows. He started to shake and reached for her. She took his hand and led him to the train station.

No one appeared to have heard the gunshots. Maybe they had but were too frightened to do anything.

CHAPTER 35

Clover led Jimmy to a bench. She put her arm around his shoulder, "Breathe deeply and try to relax."

Jimmy pulled away, lowered his head between his hands. "I'm sorry, Clover… I thought I was tougher than this."

Clover didn't speak. She put her hand on his knee and waited.

The only sound was the mumble of their fellow passengers and Jimmy's slow breathing as he took out his handkerchief and wiped his eyes.

"We have to talk, Jimmy."

"We haven't got time now. Let's board the train."

Tears ran down her cheeks. Her breath was uneven and her hands shook. She dabbed her beautiful brown eyes with a handkerchief.

"I'm not going with you."

Jimmy's face turned white. "What, after everything that happened? We almost died tonight."

"I've been living a lie. This isn't my world, Jimmy."

"I need you, Clover.

She shook her head in response.

"I've been thinking about this for a while."

"We're a team, baby. Please stay,"

"We'll always be running from the police or mobsters. What would life be like with a family? Always looking over our shoulders. I'll never forget tonight. I almost killed a man. Nothing's worth that."

"That'll change, Clover. We'll stay in Mexico and lay low. We have enough money to last us for a long, long time."

"Goddammit, Jimmy. Don't you understand? This is stolen money. I don't want any of it. I'm going to become a school teacher."

"There'll be nothing to stop you from doing whatever you want...I love you, Clover."

"Please Jimmy, don't make this harder than it is."

"Half of this sixty grand is yours."

"I don't want any of it. I'm going back to Winnipeg... I'm going home. I forgot about the important things: honor, integrity and family.

"Can't you see? Clover, I always thought I was a failure. God knows, my mother told me often enough. I'm somebody now and it's because of you."

Clover stood up, took the bag that contained the money and handed it to Jimmy. She choked up, started to walk away, then turned around. "I love you, Jimmy, but it's over."

"Jesus, Clover. Let's not end like this."

She shook her head again, this time with more conviction. Jimmy walked over and took her hand.

Clover pulled away, "It's goodbye, Jimmy."

The voice was firm, determined. She turned and didn't look back. He watched her walk away.

He hadn't felt like this since the day he sat on the bank of the lake, tears running down his cheeks, watching men dragging Minisinakwa Lake for his father's body. This was how loneliness and despair felt.

It had been all sunshine and roses back when he and Audrey left Wishart Falls for Windsor. She was running from the restricted life her parents insisted on. They'd met Ray. He was reckless, fun loving and lived for the thrills of this new era. Austerity was over and everyone was chasing something. But Ray was dead now and Jimmy didn't know what he was chasing anymore.

Jimmy thought back to how it felt to be cooped up in jail. Since then, he'd felt lucky with the gold heist, luckier still when he met Clover. But now, things had turned again. Clover was gone. Was it because of who he was and how he lived?

He knew nothing would change her mind.

He opened the bag and stared at its contents. On top of the money was Clover's dream catcher. He turned and started to follow Clover. He stopped, realizing it was over. What would this new chapter in his life bring? He had no option but to find out. He closed the bag and walked out of the station to the train.

He started singing:

She was a picture, in old Spanish lace
And for a tender while I kissed the smile, upon her face.

For it was Fiesta, and we were so gay.
Then she smiled and she whispered manyana.
Never dreaming that we were parting
And I lied as I whispered manyana, for our tomorrow never came.
South of the border, down Mexico way.

Jimmy boarded the train and sat down. He opened the bag and touched the money sitting on top of the picture of Jesus on the cross.

"You really messed up this time," Jesus said.

Jimmy had nothing to say.

This is all that was left, Clover was gone. He'd miss Bogart. He was really on his own now. For the first time in his life, whatever he was, whatever he became, was up to him. As he closed his eyes, the coach banked slightly around a curve, gathered speed. The whistle blew and the train sped west.

EPILOGUE

It's been a hell of a long time trying to forget.

Busting my ass. Trying to keep things straight. Thinking of her every night, and sometimes during the day.

What did she say once? "I love you, Jimmy." That wasn't enough for me. I let money get in the way: $60,000 worth.

There have been other women over the years. I was married once for a short time, after that it was mostly torn-down, booze-soaked ladies who charged a fee. A few who walked on the straight side, but I think they were more interested in helping me spend my money. Well, we sure did that.

Getting off the train in Los Mochis twenty years ago and looking at the strength of the breakers on the Pacific Ocean pounding the shore made me feel puny and didn't help my sorrow a damn bit. I tried to have it both ways but Clover didn't buy it.

"This way, Señor." A long passageway on a sandy path between Chiapas pine trees led to a two-room casita. A hammock stretched between trees and a table with two chairs sat on hard packed ground in the shade. The only sound was birds singing.

Damn, she would've loved this place.

"Gracias," the old guy said when I paid him for the rent and three bottles of tequila. I filled a dresser drawer with my belongings, stuffed the money under the mattress, and hung the dream catcher over the bed. The picture of Jesus on the cross was placed over a nail on the kitchen wall.

I walked out, sat in the shade, and opened a bottle of tequila.

"Wake up, Señor." A voice repeated itself until I woke, and wished I were dead. The headache and nausea was bad, a hell of a lot worse was the tightening in my chest, and the thoughts of giving up. I reached down on the side of the bed for the tequila, lifted it to my mouth; it was empty.

"I'm worried about you, Señor. Three days is a long time without food."

I opened my eyes, got up, staggered to the toilet and vomited. "I need a drink."

"I brought you one."

He handed me a cup of tequila, and set a jug of water on the floor. I was shaking too much, He held the cup to my lips and I drank, then lay on the bed and covered my head with a blanket.

"There's more in the cantina but you have to eat," he said.

I turned my head, opened one eye and looked at this Good Samaritan. Short and wiry with grey hair and needing a shave. "Gracias."

"My name is Luis." He smiled. "It's hell and only gets worse. The snakes haven't come yet. Sleep, then come to the cantina." He picked up the cup and left.

A green Cadillac bearing down, gunshots, moaning and Clover screaming echoed through chambers of gold. The chills came in waves. The blanket was wet and the smell of decay with the taste of sour alcohol brought everything home, I was one sorry-ass bastard.

The curtains were drawn and the room was dark as I sat up on the side of the bed, holding my head with my hands and my elbows resting on my knees. Finally I rose, picked up the jug and stumbled into the kitchen, glanced at Jesus and lowered my eyes. He had nothing to say.

I drank from the jug and battled to keep the water down, filled the basin, washed my face and hands and tried to comb my matted hair. I had to have a drink.

A young man in a western shirt and black sombrero was strumming a guitar and singing on a small stage, across from the bar, in the cantina.

Out in the West Texas town of El Paso,
I fell in love with a Mexican girl.
Nighttime would find me in Rosa's cantina.
Music would play and Felina would whirl.

"My name is Gabriela." The sweetest señorita in all of Mexico walked over and smiled at me.

I ordered a bottle of tequila.

"Luis said you have to eat with your drinking. He said you have the blues."

"Bring me something, I don't care what it is."

"Si Señor."

She returned with a shot glass of tequila and a bowl of chicken soup. "You have to eat before I bring more tequila."

I felt too miserable to argue. I ate.

I took a bottle of tequila back to the casita, poured a tumbler full, drank half and went to bed.

I don't know what kind of birds were singing when I opened my eyes, but they were noisy. My head felt like a lemon being squeezed and my heart was pounding like a herd of runaway mustangs. I reached for the bottle of tequila, looked at it, and put it down. Got up, grabbed about five aspirins, chewed them and went back to sleep.

The sun was high in the sky, and the birds didn't sound that loud, when I woke up the second time. I walked to the cantina and ordered chicken soup and a beer.

I married Gabriela, that sweetest señorita in all of Mexico, bought a ranch, hired Luis and raised horses. We watched her die, and buried her under the protective branches of a cottonwood tree.

Maybe it was the grey in my beard and the lines across my forehead and the sides of my face, when I looked in the mirror. I knew it was time.

I had to find Clover.

The windshield wipers on the old Dodge truck were fighting a losing battle with the early summer rains.

"When are you coming back?" Luis said as he slowed the truck to a crawl.

"Don't know."

The rain had slowed when we pulled up at the station.

"Keep the place running, Luis."

"Goodbye, Jimmy, I hope you find what you're looking for."

I shook his hand, grabbed my suitcase, hurried to the station, and bought a one-way ticket and a lower berth to Detroit. I had no idea where Clover was, but it was a start.

In the early morning of the third day the train pulled into Juarez. This is where it had ended: twenty years ago. This is where Clover turned and walked away. She didn't want the stolen money. She wanted to be a schoolteacher.

Would she have gone back to Winnipeg? How was she? Where was she?

The taxi dodged potholes. A few burnt-out shells of buildings lined the streets of Detroit. I had heard about the race riots that changed the city forever. I felt a sense of despair. The rain didn't help.

We went over the bridge to Windsor and the Bogart Smithers Jr. downtown law office. The oak door led me into a lounge with a young bright-looking secretary with a ponytail who looked up from the typewriter and smiled.

"Can I help you, sir?"

"I'd like to talk to Mr. Smithers for a few minutes."

"Do you have an appointment?"

"No. Just tell him its Jimmy Delaney."

She pressed the button on the intercom, "A Mr. Delaney to see you."

Bogart said, "Send him in." She gave me the sweetest smile.

I opened the door as Bogart rose from a mahogany desk as big as his old basement office. He walked over to me. Except for the grey hair and about twenty pounds, he looked the same. The bulge around his middle was well covered with a four hundred dollar suit.

"Jimmy." He shook my hand, stood back and laughed. Then he grabbed me in a hug. "Damn, double damn. Jesus, Jimmy, how are you?"

"I'm fine, Bogart. Now, you're looking real good."

"I came back from Santa Fe and cleaned up my act. Haven't taken a drink in a long time. Even got married."

The blood rushed from my head. I sat on a chair. "Married?"

"Yeah…an old friend of mine. I've known her from grade school."

"Congratulations," I finally said.

"I don't know your plans, Jimmy but Windsor has changed. They cleaned the place up."

I thought of Sergeant O'Connor. He was a hardnosed cop but you could depend on him to do what was right, even though he took a few shortcuts. Looks like he won.

Bogart lit up a cigar; the aroma telling me it was a Havana. "Where you been all these years?"

"Mexico."

"I think I know the reason you're here."

"Have you heard from her?"

"You broke her heart, Jimmy."

"I made a choice. The money made me somebody. I wasn't just a broken-down jailbird. My mother died knowing her son had made a pile of money."

Bogart walked back to his desk, sat and swiveled around. He stared out the window for a long time. "We kept in touch. She waited for you."

"Tell me, Bogart."

"There's not much to tell." Bogart loosened his tie, got up, and turned to me. "She came to see me, guess it was about a year after you left. She didn't look too good." He went to his desk, reached into the bottom drawer and pulled out a bottle of Canadian Club. "Want a drink, Jimmy? I haven't had one for over—"

"Christ, Bogart, tell me!"

"I'm trying to. Jesus. I loved her too. Guess you knew that. Remember the old days, Jimmy?"

Please, Bogart."

He rubbed his forehead with the palms of his hands and let out a long sigh.

"She didn't look good. She wanted money to go home. I gave her some."

"She went home?"

"That's what she said. She wasn't the same woman."

"Goddammit," I said. "What in hell do you mean?"

"I'm late for an appointment. Maybe you can call me tomorrow?" He walked to the door and opened it.

"You didn't answer my question, Bogart."

"She looked hard, brittle—"

"I'm going to find her," I said.

"Good luck."

I shook Bogart's hand and walked away. I didn't want him to see me cry.

The taxi ride down Wyandotte Street was slow. Everyone seemed to have a car and was in a race to get somewhere. I could never figure why. There wasn't a hell of a lot of action. Other than getting there first, who gives a damn? We turned onto Drouillard Road and drove by the Temple Tavern. A closed sign was in the window.

I thought of Albert sitting at his corner table sipping draft beer and holding court. He had been an inspiration to me then, one of the best safecrackers in the business and well known, revered even; among the circle of ex-cons who frequented the area.

It's too late for regrets. It won't change anything.

She said she was going home and that was a farm on the outskirts of Winnipeg: a three-day train-ride from here.

I sat in the observation car and from there looked out at the endless forest of Northern Ontario. We passed the small village of Wishart Falls and I wondered about Audrey: was she here? It's been more than two decades ago we boarded the bus, to find a life that meant something. The happiness I found was fleeting, I don't think she found any. My mother would be buried beside my father in the small cemetery. There wouldn't be anyone to visit the grave.

After a night in a berth, the dining room was welcoming and so was eating on china plates being served by waiters in white jackets. By now, the sun was shining on golden fields of wheat that melded into the sky. A few white clouds drifted aimlessly.

The sun was setting when the train pulled into Winnipeg. I booked a room at the Fort Garry Hotel and spent the evening in the bar. It didn't help. The jitters and butterflies were trying to see who would win. They ended up in a tie.

Sunday morning was quiet. The phonebook listing of the name Spence was a long one. I tore out the page with the names and addresses and went to the dining room. The waitress said that going by my list, the only Spence living out of town was the third name from the top. She drew a map.

I rented a car and drove north. Every mile seemed to turn my stomach into the victim of a scary movie. My heart was the director.

I pulled into a gravel driveway covered in weeds that led to a wooden house with a sagging roof, sitting on a slight hill. A barn, corral and a drive shed, with a few sparse trees surrounded a pond covered with brown and green scum.

I parked and walked around the corner to a veranda that ran the length of the back of the house. A small figure, covered with a red and yellow blanket, sat on a rocking chair.

"Excuse me," I said.

A woman turned to me. Her hair was white, her skin like parchment and her mouth like a pencil line. She held the sides of the chair and tried to control her shaking body.

"Mrs. Spence?"

She nodded.

"I'm looking for Clover."

"Clover?"

"Yes."

"Who are you?"

"My name is Jimmy Delaney. I'm a friend."

"I heard of you." She looked at me with bitterness. "More than I cared."

"I'm looking for her."

"She's not here.

When she pointed to the other rocking chair I sat down and waited for her to go on.

"She came home years ago. Her grandfather was gone but her father was still alive. She didn't stay long." Tears started running down her cheeks. "The only time she seemed happy was when she was racing her horse across the fields."

"Have you heard from her?" I held my breath. "Where is she? You have to tell me."

"Everything's gone. Empty barns and a dried well. You know I was born here. Oh, we had happy times. Our people would come from miles around. We would play music, dance, sing and feast on buffalo meat and corn."

"Do you know where she went?" I asked.

"West. Beyond the mountains."

"Did she say where?"

She smiled and looked up at the sky. "They're waiting for me," she said.

When I opened the small bag I carried and handed her the dream catcher, she sighed and reached for it.

"This belongs to Clover."

"So it does," she said. "She loved you."

The sun was almost set and a slight breeze was starting to blow. I rose from the rocking chair and walked to the car.

Who knows how long it takes before a heart either breaks or turns to stone but I did know I had to find her so I pointed the car west and I drove on.

Made in the USA
Charleston, SC
26 September 2015